PRAISE FOR *HOMECOMING*

"A wrenching account of the effects of war on the spirit and the heart. Tightly spun with raw emotion, *Homecoming* succeeds in encompassing a totality of humanity. . . . Expertly and effortlessly rendered, Radojčić's tangible descriptions never falter, and the reader, like Halid, is kept within its walls until the tragic end."

—*The Philadelphia Inquirer*

"[A] stunning debut . . . The novel's rare, unvarnished portrait of village life and its inexorable march toward a grim showdown make it worthy of comparison to García Márquez's *Chronicle of a Death Foretold.*"

—*Publishers Weekly*

"A fascinating glimpse into a truly foreign culture."

—*Booklist*

"Radojčić has pulled off something rarely seen in contemporary fiction: a tragedy. *Homecoming* is a disturbing, deeply persuasive work, rife with fascinating detail about a part of the world that's still quite mysterious to most Americans."

—Jennifer Egan, author of *Look at Me* and *The Invisible Circus*

"*Homecoming* takes you into a world of such truth and detail, such division and humanity, that it will never leave you."

—Gloria Steinem

"Radojčić debuts compellingly with vivid images of postwar futility as a Muslim soldier, returning to his Bosnian village, finds it impossible to escape his or his country's demons. . . . A dark and well-executed tale with unsettling scenes and the grit of reality—as well as an acute sense of loss at the failure of a good but desperate man."

—*Kirkus Reviews*

"*Homecoming* calls to mind novels like Tayeb Salih's *Season of Migration to the North* and Meja Mwangi's *Going Down River Road,* works that explore the ambivalent parameters of home. The stark beauty of the novel lies in its depiction of war as a quotidian phenomenon—something people learn to live with among the ruins—and as an unavoidable reality that confirms people's suspicions about each other."

—*Rain Taxi*

"Old Testament and Greek Tragedy played out among the Serbs and the Muslims. A tale of loss—lost lives, lost dreams, lost hope—*Homecoming* will break your heart, but you'll be thankful for the experience."

—Marcia Gillespie, *Ms.* magazine

ABOUT THE AUTHOR

Natasha Radojčić was born in Belgrade. In her early twenties, on her own, she came to New York City, earned an MFA in fiction writing from Columbia University, and stayed. She is the author of *You Don't Have to Live Here.*

HOMECOMING

HOMECOMING

A NOVEL

Natasha Radojčić

RANDOM HOUSE
TRADE PAPERBACKS
NEW YORK

2005 Random House Trade Paperback Edition

Copyright © 2002 by Natasha Radojčić-Kane
Reading group guide copyright © 2005 by Random House, Inc.

This work was originally published in hardcover by Four Walls Eight Windows in 2002. This edition published by arrangement with Four Walls Eight Windows.

LIBRARY OF CONGRESS CATALOGING-IN-PUBLICATION DATA
Radojčić, Natasha
   Homecoming : a novel/by Natasha Radojčić
     p. cm.
   ISBN 0-8129-7241-4
    1. Yugoslav War, 1991–1995—Bosnia and Hercegovina—
Fiction.   2. Yugoslav War, 1991–1995—Veterans—Fiction.
3. Bosnia and Hercegovina—Fiction.   4. Villages—Fiction.
5. Muslims—Fiction.   I. Title
   PS3618.A355 H66 2002
   813'.6—dc21   2002023166

Random House website address: www.atrandom.com

Printed in the United States of America

9 8 7 6 5 4 3 2 1

To Mom, Susan,

and Dragan Stenek

for teaching me

Truth and Rights

ACKNOWLEDGMENTS

I wish to thank Jane Abitanta, Giulia Aborio, Denise Azira, Kathryn Belden, Roberto Calasso, Matteo Codignola, Jasminka Dimović, David Ebershoff, Jennifer Egan, Marcia Gillespie, Stephanie Higgs, Daniel Menaker, John Oakes, Dr. Angelo Paiano, Borislav Radojčić, Lenore and Lee Robins, Emilie Stewart, Sadika and Smail Švraka, the Vejzagić family, and Jane Zalman. Without their tireless efforts and collaboration, I never would have been able to finish.

Some travel alongside my life requiring only a first name: Angelo, Angie, Bojana, Christine, Chuck, D., Djordje, Em, Giulia, Igor, Janer, JBZ, Marcia, Matteo, Max, Nuna, Olja, Pep, Rachel, Sakeena, Sally Shiggs, Sue, Teča, and Tetka. You all have an extraordinary talent for hope!

Finally, I wish to make note of the many anonymous, faceless, but unforgotten victims of injustices that human beings inflict upon one another. Your flourishing, despite unspeakable suffering, humbles me, inspires me, and gives me the courage and reason to persevere.

I thank you all.

HOMECOMING

1

A FAT PEASANT WOMAN, A RARITY FOR
wartime, kicked her bloated leg against the cage stuffed with
white chickens, yelling *shoo, shoo* to prevent the birds from
huddling together and keeping whatever breeze there was
from cooling them off. Each time she hit the cage her colossal
pink and purple cleavage bobbled from side to side, almost
swallowing the thick gold chain between her breasts. The pet-
rified birds clustered closer, cocking their crimson-crested
heads and their long white necks away from the attacking

limb. By the next sundown, the townsfolk would finish picking out which of the offered birds were juicy and plump enough to adorn their break-of-the-Ramadan-fast feasts. The chosen heads and necks would be separated by the *chakija*'s curved blades.

Rough red skin circled the empty yellow blankness of the birds' pupils. Somewhere Halid had read about the direct link between chickens and dinosaurs. Like him, they were descendants of magnificent warriors, and like him they hadn't an inkling of courage left.

It was too hot for early October, and he had sweated through his wool turtleneck during the three-hour bus ride from the train station in Split, where he had arrived from Sarajevo. He had spent the night crunched up on a wooden bench in the waiting room, using his suitcase as a pillow. Not having showered in over two weeks, he was embarrassed to take off his sweater. On top of the smell, he had no undershirt, and the fresh skin of his scar might make the other passengers uneasy. Well, he thought, evaluating the traveling conditions of his caged companions, at least I'm not covered with feathers.

"I heard you tell the driver that you're just back from the war," the young man sitting next to him commented. "What's it like, Sarajevo?"

"It used to be big," Halid said, hoping that his answer would shut the young man up. "Now it's just burnt."

"I'm going to go there. The trade schools are reopening next month. In two years I'll be a licensed electrician."

"Congratulations."

Halid's village was approaching. Soon he would be getting off. All he had to do was ignore the intruder a little longer, so he pretended to be more interested in the sights outside the bus window.

The familiar turns on the narrow two-lane road pushed through the Dinara. The thick mountain forest separated the harsh *rakija*-brandy-guzzling highlanders from the docile coastal dwellers. To Halid's left lay an empty water channel, one of the many failed Communist ventures. It was designed in the late seventies to bring water after the ten-year drought had destroyed several harvests. The leading local Communist politician, a self-proclaimed "loyal son of the dry land," concocted a plan to blast through the fields that bordered the road and carve out a water channel. Almost everyone in the area lived off the land and had been reduced to total poverty by the drought. The young men, including Halid, volunteered to work on the channel, which got them out of high school classes and paid their keep for two months.

The project resulted in several blunders. The worst was the government's decision to confiscate the land around the channel for "security purposes." When the fresh water finally arrived and took care of the drought, most people had little land left to farm and no real access to the water.

Halid wondered to whom the cornfields and empty pastures belonged now that the war was over. The Communists were no longer in power, and the new land distribution was in effect. He wondered if any of his family's cattle had survived the war. Five years later, with all the heavy stable work falling on his mother's ailing back, he couldn't hope for much.

Mother. He hadn't called in months. They had never been able to afford a phone, and he was too embarrassed to call the neighbors and wait while somebody fetched her. Sweet Mother: she wrote every month. At first he opened her letters eagerly, but there was nothing in them except news of someone's death. She never complained of her own sorry state—and not for lack of suffering, which was obvious in the scribbles and corrections. Her hand shook in deep sadness. After five months, he stopped reading. The rest of the forty-eight letters remained neatly folded at the bottom of his suitcase, tied with a ribbon he washed each time a new one arrived.

THE BUS DRIVER WAS UNDER PRESSURE TO GET TO HIS last stop before nightfall. He barely slowed down to let Halid jump off. There were still Serbian rebel snipers everywhere, especially on the desolate mountain roads that were not patrolled by the Bosnian Army. Their infamous "check-points" were often the sites of robberies.

The driver shouted, "Good luck to you, hero," as he accelerated, leaving Halid in a cloud of dust.

He kicked his heels together to shake off his boots and dropped his suitcase. He opened and closed his fist a few times, pumping the blood back into his fingers. The platoon doctor swore it was the best therapy. Three months after the bullet had been removed from his shoulder, the pain could get almost as intense as the day he was shot.

He sat down on his suitcase and tossed the sweater on the road before him. The night was descending quickly, and it brought a slight refreshing breeze. He lifted his arms to air out his armpits.

The middle of the road before him was torn up, probably by a military truck, or even a tank. But the scattered acorns were untouched—Halid figured it had to have been peaceful here for at least two weeks. With his good hand, he picked up a handful of pebbles. They had cracks from water freezing and expanding inside them. They had been on the road for a while, possibly a winter or two. Maybe he even stepped on one of them when he departed four years ago. That thought stirred him, and he let the stones roll out of his hand.

He wasn't ready for this. He had not planned to come back. He had not planned to be here, not this soon. The doctor prescribed another three months of therapy before he was to go home. After the treatment, he intended to stay in Sarajevo with one of his Muslim war buddies whose Christian wife left him and took their children back to her father in Serbia. But the ambulances brought in more wounded than the hospital could handle, and he was asked to clear the space.

"So, you were shot?" the nurse asked when he objected. "So was everybody else." She handed him his suitcase without looking up from a new admission sheet.

During the first few days he slept in an abandoned building, hiding from the military police who were rounding up the wandering soldiers and sending them home to their families. He rang his friend's doorbell several times at night; there was no answer. He tried getting a job cleaning stores for the local merchants. They laughed at him in his uniform at first, but when they realized he was serious, asked for his ID: only locals could be hired. Then armed guards were placed in front of all abandoned buildings, leaving nowhere to hide. The only option left was home, the last place in the world he wanted to see.

ANXIOUS, HE LIT A MARLBORO. SMOKING WAS A NEW habit he picked up in the infirmary. The wounded soldiers around him claimed that they gladly took bullets " 'cause there are always plenty of Marlboros around the hospital." So, he tried one and liked it.

Usually inhaling smoke helped release tension. No such luck this time. It wasn't fear that troubled him. He had faced fear during the ceaseless shelling. No, this was different. The whole area seemed strangely distant.

He looked down at the road. Another dry season. The acorns were terribly brittle. As a child, whenever his soccer team lost, he'd crush a few or stump over dry patches of soil to calm himself. Now, there was only a single acorn close enough for his boot to reach. He went for it. The sudden burst under his sole broke his uneasiness. Even the tingling in

8

his arm subsided. He stubbed out his cigarette on the ground and continued toward the house.

What was once his grandfather's plum orchard, now the property of the Communist government's jam factory, stretched on his left all the way to the house, almost half a mile farther down. Halid's family never stopped referring to it as "our orchard." Father called it "my fucking stolen plums," which was almost always followed by a hardy spit. It was the only instance Father's unshakable faith in the Communist confiscation practices faltered slightly.

As Father grew more attached to the bottle and less to anything else, Halid spent days in the orchard hiding from the troubles liquor bestows upon a family. When Father discovered his son's passion for plums, he tried bribing Halid to sneak home a bag or two from time to time. "And why not?" he asked when Mother subtly suggested that stealing from the government might not be the wisest idea. "Those are my fucking plums." And he spat, of course.

The plums had not been picked this year—no surprise, with all the men away—and Halid could see them, dark, overripe, and rotting on the ground. A waste of good brandy.

While he was stationed outside Sarajevo, he often worried his house might have been bombed or burned and that the orchard had been cut down to make room for the wheat fields. As the new Muslim volunteers from this area enlisted, they all brought along the good news: his village had been spared.

His house was one of five, three on the left, two on the right, separated by a cattle path that stretched all the way to the stream half a mile farther. From afar his house didn't seem to have changed. The broad stone building with a terrace connecting all four windows of the top floor had lost its original splendor long before this last war. Once upon a time it was the proud residence of generations of Vejzagics. The distinguished Muslim family ruled over the local Serbian peasants in the name of the Ottoman Empire, and his highness the Sultan, with generosity and wisdom for almost three hundred years. One of the early family fathers who was awarded the title *bey* for distinguished war efforts in the early eighteenth century, planted seven poplars around the main house, symbolizing the seven sons he had with his first wife. Now the gigantic trees dwarfed the house, casting a perpetual shade. Some of their leaves had grown even larger than the windows.

The house had been set on fire back in the twenties. A slighted relative felt cheated out of some corn, and thirsty for revenge, hid a dynamite stick inside a fire log. Thanks to a stroke of good fortune, no one was near the fire when the log blew up. The old stone hearth and the chimney were sturdy enough to withstand the explosion, but the flames spread throughout the rest of the house, destroying the entire first floor and most of the second. When the house was rebuilt, a separate kitchen was added to the barn across from the main house. The old hearth was sealed shut and the kindling kept inside the living room, far away from any vengeful hands. Just in case.

Mother probably used only one room now that she was alone. Even when the electricity was working, she couldn't bear the expense of heating more than one. Now he would have to get a job and help. It was certainly his duty, and yet he couldn't imagine entering the small damp rooms of his dilapidated family home.

Across the road from Halid's home, above a badly piled haystack, the flat roof of another house was just visible: a grubby concrete building that once housed the dairy serfs and cheese and butter processing equipment. After the Austrians freed the serfs, they were allowed to stay and live in the houses. Then the Communists came and brought along the principles of the Red revolution: property for the poor. Now a *Kaur*, a Serbian family, great-grandchildren of the serfs—the Milosnics—owned it. Momir, the eldest of the Milosnic children, had fought for the other side and stepped on a mine during a night raid on Sarajevo, dying instantly.

Momir had also been Halid's best and oldest friend. The kind of friend who would hold a secret encouraging grip on Halid's eight-year-old hand when, during a schoolwide lice infestation, all the children were ordered to shave their heads. Halid squirmed in the barber's chair, terrified that the nasty clippers would ravage his head instead of killing off the typhoid-carrying insects. If it weren't for Momir, Halid would have been tied to the chair like a girl—the worst shame imaginable.

During the war he thought of Momir as a soldier and a grown man first. Standing on guard one freezing February night, he overheard two soldiers from his platoon report that some Serb "went break dancing" in the minefield. It wasn't until two weeks later, during the POW exchange, that he learned from a captured Christian who served under Momir, that his major wandered onto the "Muslim wall-to-wall carpeting," Serbian slang for mines, and "met the Maker."

Death surrounded Halid then: young, old, cruel, quick, ugly, deserved, unexpected, hoped for, but the news of Momir uncovered a whole new category: the death of a best friend.

Only one window on Momir's house faced the road, and Halid could not resist the temptation to peek in and see how the family had managed over the last four years. Through the grime, he saw a long water basin built more than a hundred years ago to water the dairy cattle that had shared the quarters with the serfs. Later that basin became a sink, and now pots, pans, and large cooking utensils hung on the hooks nailed into the windowpane above the sink. The mind is a funny thing as it gets older, he thought; he never would have noticed utensils before.

A woman with her back turned to Halid and her hair wrapped with a black scarf to show that she was widowed had just finished washing the dishes. She wiped her hands on a rag and reached over the basin's edge on the tip of her toes to grab a baking pan. There was something recognizable in the way her elongated arms reached much higher than one would anticipate from someone rather short. When she turned around and placed the pan onto the huge wooden table, he discerned her face. It was Mira.

He had loved her once. But he had been too young to go against his family's wishes. She was a penniless Christian girl, destined to poverty, with no chance of ever crossing his good Muslim family's doorstep wearing wedding ornaments. Halid knew this long before she did. "It's a good thing she is pretty and healthy and can haul all day long," Mother commented on Mira's strong constitution, totally oblivious to her son's feelings for the lovely *Kaur.* "Her father'll be able to dump her on someone." And he did—after months of negotiating with Momir's mother, Stana, Mira's father finally managed to convince the proud Milosnic matriarch to accept the destitute beauty.

How she has withered, Halid thought. Her face was colorless, her lips drawn into a taut line. The life around here aged people so fast. She looked spent and tiny in the ramshackle kitchen. Mira adjusted her scarf and unveiled the thinning hair at her temples. Hunger, he knew: starvation. It was Mira's unusually beautiful hair that had first attracted him back in high school. Heavy and blond, "too blond for a *Kaur* peasant," as Mother pointed out, her mane charmed him. She used to twist it into several thick braids, which she would then secure at the back of her head with a plastic clip. "Too poor for anything better than plastic," Halid's aunt added maliciously. An expensive copper clip was the first present Halid ever gave her.

He pressed his fist against his chest and leaned his forehead against the window. Breathe, he reminded himself. Breathe. Then he reached with his hand as if he could touch the image before him and realized that his hand was shaking. He quickly shoved it in his pocket. He was never cut out for this place.

Somewhere across the nearby stream a dog barked. A young dog, probably. Nothing got old around here. It started to get dark, and he could now hear more dogs barking all over the mountain. The wolves must be close. This will be a hard winter.

The mountain grew quiet. He closed his eyes and enjoyed the sounds of the evening. Then a tingle in his arm reminded him of his nakedness, of how ridiculous it would look if somebody were to see him.

A SMALL CAR DROVE UP THE ROAD AND PARKED IN FRONT of the first house at the village's entrance. The people who used to live there were old friends, *Kaurs* like Momir. Halid hunted many times with the head of the family, Savo. He was an excellent shot, famous for hitting a razor, skinny side up, from a hundred feet. But he fathered no sons, nobody to protect the house, and they were forced to leave.

Their girls had excellent vegetable-growing skills, and their large, bright pumpkins were so scrumptious that Halid's aunt, a universally accepted pie queen, pronounced them "makers of heaven out of mortal seeds." The youngest daughter was a soloist in the local choir. She sang every Friday night during the summer when the villagers gathered to bake and grind coffee beans for the following week. As she accompanied her voice by the rhythmic shaking of the roasting pot, she threw amorous glances over the fire at Halid. Unfortunately, her innocent plan to lure the *bey*'s only grandson into her web backfired: the beautiful mountain summer night, and the exquisite soprano filling up the apple grove, had only intensified Halid's desire for Mira's wild mane.

The garden around the house was completely different now. No more bean stalks that grew as high as three feet in the front, and even higher in back of the house.

An unfamiliar man jumped out of the car and hurried up the stairs. Somebody must have moved into an available house. It happened all the time nowadays.

"Vulture," Halid mumbled, wishing he could throw a stone and break the window.

The sound of a child crying drifted through Mira's window, and he rose carefully. Wherever there are children, there are always bullets to protect them. He silently unlatched his suitcase and pulled his Luger out. He had left it packed so as not to scare the people on the bus. Although he hadn't shot the gun in three months, it was strange not to feel it hanging off his belt.

He peeked through the window more cautiously than before. Two small arms reached up from under the wooden table. The boy squirmed. Mira knelt down and caressed his hair until he went back to sleep. Mother had never mentioned anything about the child's birth in the few letters he had read, and he had not dared ask. Knowing Mother, all his efforts to get the information would have been useless. The old mummy could keep a secret better than any trained soldier.

On the wall behind Mira there was a large white crucifix. That was new too. The head of a bear Momir shot with a single bullet used to hang there during the more normal days.

It was strange to see Mira with a child. There was a gentleness about her he hadn't seen before. The boy grabbed the corner of the scarf and she smiled. A tinge of jealousy rippled through Halid's stomach; she had never approached him with such tenderness.

Mira stood up and cracked two eggs into a pan, stirring as a lefty would, backward. Halid smiled. Back in their school days she was constantly in trouble with the schoolteachers for writing with her left hand. They went so far as to tie her left arm to the chair to impose the proper right-hand rule upon her. There was no commanding Mira; she picked up the pencil with her mouth and scribbled all over her notebooks. After she spent five days in detention, the teachers had to lay their weapons down and abandon the idea of converting the unruly girl. Mira was inducted as the first legal lefty in the town's history.

She opened a midnight-blue box of Danish cookies

adorned with pictures of dashingly uniformed soldiers kissing the hands of beautiful young ladies in expensive Western European crinoline dresses. The metal boxes were terribly popular among the villagers. They were used to store jewelry or other precious family articles. The boxes were smuggled from Italy and sold for steep prices on the black market. Eight years ago, Mira's box had cost Halid two full-grown turkeys.

Then he realized—she had saved his box instead of pawning it, and he straightened his back, as if he had been caught slumming on watch duty by a senior officer. No doubt she needed money. Everything about her suggested dire straits: the pitiful state of the kitchen, the filth on the windows. Maybe she remembered him and thought of him often too.

Mira poured some flour from the box into the baking pan. Only a few spoonfuls came out. She opened the kitchen cupboard and found only a half-pound box of sugar and some yeast. Halid wanted to knock on the window, but he knew he should not. It would be an inappropriate time for him to speak to her. She was newly widowed, with a child by her feet. He couldn't remember how long the customary mourning lasted for a Christian woman, but he was certain that Mira's would be the longest. Stana, Momir's mother and Mira's mother-in-law, was notorious for her fanatical enforcement of the severest Orthodox rules. It would be prudent to wait. And he knew he didn't have the nerve to face Mira. He put on his sweater, picked up his suitcase, and left.

CLOSE TO HIS HOUSE THERE WAS A DESERTED CONSTRUCTION
site. Days before the first grenade blew off the top of the local
mosque, Halid came to pay respects at the house blessing. It
was the last event to which the Christians and the Muslims
came together, although they stood separately and each man
showed up with a rifle slung over his shoulder. There were
talks of war. Momir had grown pensive and gloomy over the
last weeks. When he disappeared a week later, Halid realized
that he had already volunteered to go to Sarajevo.

At the house blessing, a rooster had been sacrificed over
the freshly dug foundation. The bird's headless body ran
blindly from one side to the other, smashing into the walls of
the trench, as was preferred in the blessing ceremony—each
time the rooster hit the ground added a decade to the house's
life. Then the blood gushing from the severed neck's artery
poured over the edge of the foundation onto the surrounding
grass. The village women immediately started nudging one
another, whispering that the house was doomed. The men
walked away, concerned about a lot more than a rotten foundation.

During the war, the mud slid over the edges and almost
completely covered the hole. Reluctant to turn around and
face his house, Halid stepped over the dry mud. Mother had
been alone for a long time. What would he find? He closed
his eyes and wished himself miles away, when a picture of

Mira's bald temples appeared before him. He wondered if her teeth had fallen out. Hunger struck hair and teeth at the same time: too much rice, and nothing else.

Then he looked up. His house had aged badly. The roof sagged and the shingles had cracked. The outside clay walls used to be painted white every spring. Now they were peeling in long strips, gray from chimney soot and swollen with moisture bubbles. The eaves were dark brown with rust from the leaking gutters. They would need expensive reinforcement soon. It was too late in the rainy season to work on the house. The door hinge was missing a screw on one side and was dangling. The old rosebush was leafless and dry. Halid emptied his water jug on the soil around the bush. The water lingered on the surface.

Mother would cry as soon as she saw him. Then she would alarm the whole town. Then all their relatives and friends would arrive bringing welcoming offerings: dry meats and goat cheese, fresh roasts and rice, potato pies, pickled peppers, stuffed cabbage, loads of sweets. No matter how poor and hungry everyone had been, a man's return from winning the war was cause to bring forth the last of the food supplies. Besides, from now on the hero would provide. Gaping children would gather around his feet to hear the war stories they would later reenact in their beds, ripping a feather pillow or two before they exhausted themselves to sleep. Older relatives, those who had their own war stories, would ask considerate questions. What was it like to be in the trenches with all this new heavy artillery? Was he protected from the snipers? Had he killed anyone?

How could he admit that it was awful, that he was scared the entire time, that he could still taste the gunpowder in his mouth, and that every day he thought of Malik, who was shot in the head while eating next to Halid in the trenches. The bloodstain had washed out of Halid's clothes, but the oil stain from Malik's soup remained on his sweater. Halid was not in the mood for war stories, not yet. His neck was hurting and his arm had gone to sleep again. The front door looked uninviting. He hid his suitcase behind the rosebush and headed back toward the town.

2

THERE HAD BEEN ONLY MARGINAL STREET
fighting in Halid's town. What would later qualify as the war
between the Serbian paramilitary and the Muslim Resistance
started as a bar brawl between the members of the Serbian
and Muslim soccer teams and their fans. On one side there
were the Serbs led by their goalie and a temporary team captain. Momir had been the real captain, but he had already
shipped off to Sarajevo for the "real war." On the other, the
Muslims and several Catholic Croats. The Catholics feared

their homes would be wrecked and their daughters raped by the rowdy Serbs, so they sided with the Muslims to increase their numbers.

The dispute started over a penalty kick against the Serbs that led to the only goal in the game and their loss. Incensed, the Serbs refused to shake hands with the winners, the first sign of impending trouble. Then, they retreated to "their tavern." For months while preparing for war, the government secretly ordered people of different religions to drink separately. Drunks were harder to control.

That evening, not even the most persuasive infiltrator could convince the angry fans that the Serbian judge, "the traitor of his own blood" who called the penalty against the Serbs, wasn't on Istanbul's payroll. Serbs demolished the "Muslim" tavern an hour later. In retaliation, the Muslims set a police car on fire, and the armed conflict escalated out of control.

The Serbs managed to smuggle a long-range M109 howitzer tank from the army camp across the river. One of them was an excellent shot, and right after he hit the mosque's minaret, he struck the general store. A perfect shot, so rare in artillery fire, dug a tunnel straight through the first floor. The top two floors had no fire marks, but the twelve identical windows were all shattered.

The rest of the main street, which connected the bus stop on one end with the town's biggest tavern on the other, remained untouched. Buildings occupied one side, the Dumanija River the other. Past the tavern, where the concrete sidewalk disappeared and the cobblestones started, the road snaked around the ravine that the Dumanija dug between the two surrounding mountains in its more glorious days—when it was rich with water. In recent years, it would dry up by mid-June and become home for beehives, spiders, and mosquitoes.

Right before the war, the townsfolk tried to chase the insects out with smoke, but some dry shrubs caught fire and within minutes the flames raged up to the tower that overlooked the ravine. The flames scorched the walls and destroyed the famous weeping willow that grew inside the tower. The willow was legendary. As a rite of passage, young men climbed the slippery moss-covered walls in order to cut off a branch and carve out a whistle whose clear sound was celebrated far beyond the town's borders, and a particularly good whistle made it all the way to Istanbul, to the holiest of all lips, those of the Imam. The townsfolk considered the death of the tree a tragedy. The peasants went even further, saying it was a terrible omen. Something bad was about to happen.

And it did. At first the fighting went around the town limits, staying mostly in the villages, going from one cluster of peasants' houses to the other. The night shots disturbed the townsfolk's sleep, but they all remained at home comforting themselves with the idea that all this hubbub was some peasant business that would be over as soon as the army arrived.

After the minaret was damaged and the general store destroyed, the merchants closed their doors and left town, hoping the war would be over soon.

LOOKING AT THE ABANDONED STORES AND BROKEN windows overwhelmed Halid. Nothing had prepared him for what seeing his town would feel like. Some of the soldiers talked to mullahs right before they were sent home. He left in a hurry. Besides, his father had believed in Communism. He did not, but he found no comfort in the mullahs' teaching. He understood little. At the hospital, the fatally wounded showed most interest in the otherwise inexplicable religious customs. Halid thought it a death panic. Now, staring at a fountain with the head of a lion missing half his mane and a part of his chin spitting water, he wasn't so sure he was right. On his own he didn't have the tools required for a homecoming.

In the shadow of the fountain, inside a large plastic bucket, sat a young Gypsy boy, not over ten or eleven years old. He probably used to fill the bucket with soapy water and wait at the parking lot for the car owners to let him clean their windshields. There hadn't been any gas for months, therefore no cars to wash. Sitting inside the empty bucket with his feet dangling, the boy looked as if he were going to the bathroom. Halid smiled at him and asked, "Is anything coming out?"

"Fuck you," the boy said.

He had dug out a square on the ground with a hole in the middle, and he aimed for the hole with his marbles.

"Allah Hue Giber. Allah Hue Giber," the mullah sang as loud as a grenade, calling for the evening prayer. The noise startled the boy, and he dropped a ginger-colored "metal-hitter" before he had a good chance to aim. The marble bounced off a rock and tumbled down the street straight into the sewer.

"Shit, shit," the boy shouted. He jumped out of the bucket and stomped his foot on the ground. "Help," he yelled at Halid. "Help."

There was nothing appealing about the idea of crawling inside the sewer for a marble, but he felt bad for the boy. Back when he owned a car he always yelled at "the goddamn darkies" to leave his car alone and not make a mess of his windshield, which he now regretted. The war had made a wimp out of him, he realized, loaded him with remorse. He pulled a bill out of his pocket and gave it to the boy.

"Here. You can buy a marble factory with this."

The boy gawked at the bill in his hand. It was a German ten-mark bill, possibly the first he had ever seen, and without picking up the rest of his marbles, or thanking Halid, he ran away.

The tavern stood exactly as it had before the war: the big wooden door, the huge spittoon next to it, and a metal bench for the overly intoxicated to nap before they stumbled home. It belonged to a friend, Shukri, with whom Momir and Halid had hunted since they were boys. Like Halid, Shukri loved Momir.

Shukri was not blessed with any talent for sports and was teased incessantly at school, which battered his spirit and made him bitter and stingy. But he was a hard worker and a loyal son who took good care of his mother and his younger brother. So even with his shortcomings, he was welcomed in everybody's homes. When the war started Shukri stayed back for a while but eventually enlisted as a cook. Since the trials of trench warfare and Momir's death had taught Halid humility, he eagerly accepted Shukri as a close friend. He was transferred and eventually sent home six months before Halid was released.

Inside, a heavy whiff of tobacco and plum brandy greeted Halid. Maybe ten men sat around smoking and drinking. When Shukri recognized him, he stood up and walked toward Halid with open arms. He had gotten skinnier and his skin was darker, rougher. His face smelled of pipe.

"Al-hamdu lillah. Praise the Lord," Shukri said, smiling. "Our hero is back. Salaam Alekum, Halid. Come and sit right here and eat with me. Let's have some food."

"Alekum Salaam, Shukri," Halid replied.

"How is your mother?" Shukri asked when Halid sat down.

"I came here first."

"Is that so? She could use some good news, with all your cousins gone."

"Plenty of time for that. I wanted some *rakija* first."

"*Rakija?*" Shukri raised his eyebrows. "I don't remember you ever touching the bottle."

"Time changes a man, Shukri." Halid put his hand on the bar, firmly signaling he was not about to endure a lecture.

"I'll drink to that." Shukri understood and opened a fresh bottle. "Smell it. It's heavenly. Almost twenty-five years old. My father baked five barrels the year my brother was born."

"My God," Halid laughed. "He's twenty-five?"

"Yeah. And this is one of the last bottles I have left. Zhiveli."

The sharp sound of glass hitting glass reminded Halid of the peace. In the trenches nobody toasted loudly: the snipers were always listening.

"I saw your mother as much as I could since I came back, chopped her wood," Shukri said.

"Thank you."

"She sold a cow to pay for help with the crop. But the harvests have been ruined with too much rain. Makes you wonder why we fought the Serbs."

Halid said nothing.

"She has suffered a lot, you know. Every time I see her she looks older."

The flutters in Halid's stomach awakened, and he threw down his drink to silence them. He reached for the bottle to pour the next one.

"What do you intend to do now? You'll have to start plowing right away if you want to catch up with the weather."

"I'd like to finish this drink in peace," Halid said.

Shukri's face tensed and he stood up. "Suit yourself. But know that a man drinking by himself is nobody's friend."

Soon Halid's fingers greased the glass for the third time, and he tossed fifty pfennigs inside the copper tip jar. He used the moment when Shukri went into the cellar to leave without saying goodbye.

THE BAKERY, WHICH HAD NOT BEEN DAMAGED, WAS NEXT door to the tavern. Rade the baker was a Serb, but he was a clever and crafty man who married a Muslim woman and gave his children Muslim names. Unlike in Serbia, where Muslim names carried a stigma, in Bosnia they were favored. Around here people still remembered the time Muslims owned everything.

A bell chimed when Halid opened the door. Rade dropped the bread crates on the floor and offered his hand as soon as he saw him.

"Salaam Alekum, Halid. Good to see you back."

"Alekum Salaam, Rade, how are the boys?"

"Aferim, healthy, and still too young to fight. We heard from your mother that you were shot."

"It's healing."

"Do you think it's really over?"

"It is for me."

Halid bought a cheese pie, *burek*. Then he asked, "Rade, how much flour do you have in the store?"

Rade looked up, confused, "Ten bags, I think. Fifty pounds each. Why?"

"How much for a bag?"

"I don't sell them."

"How much anyway?"

"One hundred."

"Can you drop three by the Milosnic house? I'll come by in the morning and pay you three hundred."

"What do you mean?"

"You heard me."

Halid knew that Rade never sold flour to his customers. He bought it from his brother-in-law, who ran a Communist Party–controlled mill and sold falsely marked "reject" bags at a discounted price to Rade, who made a huge profit baking the bread at almost no cost. But he was also sure that Rade wouldn't refuse him—the war hero with a gun strapped to his belt was the authority around here. A bag of cheaply purchased flour was not worth risking the store.

"I'll see that it gets done tonight," Rade said reluctantly.

"Thank you. And . . . don't tell them it's from me. They may not take it. Tell them you were going over your books and you realized you owed them some money, so you're giving them flour instead."

"A hundred and fifty pounds of flour is a big mistake. They'll be suspicious."

"Come on, Rade, they're all women there. They'll be happy to take it. I'll settle the bill in the morning."

THE CHILL IN THE AIR AND THE STARLESS SKY THAT
settled over the ravine warned of a storm. Shukri could
always predict the weather. It wasn't right, the way he just
left; they were friends after all.

The chairs in the tavern's garden were leaned against the
tables and chained to secure them from being knocked over,
or stolen. One table was untied, the chairs moved back, and
there were chewing gum wrappers on the ground around it.
The sight of the thin chair legs reminded him of the interro-
gation rooms where he spent countless hours with prisoners.
No useful information was extracted from these sessions:
only pained silences, crying and begging. This was not a war
where real strategies were used. There were no secrets to be
revealed.

An older man, unfamiliar to Halid, hosed the pavement
in front of the tavern. He looked at Halid, annoyed.

"We're closing."

"It's still early."

"We are just the same."

"I'm Shukri's friend," Halid said.

"He's gone to get something."

"I have time."

"Damn drunks," the old man grumbled into his beard.

"Where are you from?" Halid asked.

"Bijeljina."

It was the town in the area Serbs "cleansed" as soon as the war started, rendering most Muslims homeless.

"Did the Serbs turn you out of the house?"

The old man didn't answer. He clenched his jaw proudly and continued. Halid had insulted him. Maybe he hadn't always been a sweep.

"Where are you living now?"

"Shukri lets me stay in the basement." He paused and then added, "I don't drink. Ever."

When he was finished, he folded the hose and left. Loud thunder erased the sound of his footsteps, and the first raindrops splashed against Halid's face. The rain grew heavy and his sweater was immediately drenched.

From the other side of the street he saw an open umbrella charging directly toward him. As it reached the first tables, Halid recognized the Gypsy boy's face grinning through the curtain of the pouring rain. He was barefoot and the wind inside the umbrella almost lifted him off the ground.

"Need an umbrella?" he asked Halid. "Cheap."

"How much?"

"Ten marks."

Halid peeled off one soppy bill.

"Here."

The boy unwrapped the wadded bill with his dirty hand and looked at Halid.

"This is only a mark."

"Take the rest from the marble money."

"Fuck you." The boy spat on the ground by Halid's feet. He closed the umbrella under his armpit and jetted away, vaulting the silver puddles. Halid laughed out loud. Once, he had stolen what he thought was brand-new eye shadow from some salesman's fake alligator bag and had run away in the same manner. The round turquoise box turned out to be a used sample. Mira tossed the box away, appalled at the thought of the thousands of god-knows-who that may have touched it before.

"Hey, hero, what are you getting wet for?" Shukri appeared in front of Halid. "Are you nuts?"

"Look how clean the rain is." Halid stuck his palm up, showing the drops bouncing off of it. "Shining like a brand-new bullet. No mud around it."

"So, you have gone nuts. Well, at least you're in a better mood. Let's go inside," Shukri said as he unlocked the tavern gate.

"Did you eat anything?" Halid asked.

"No."

"Here, let's share this." He slammed a bundle of greasy paper on the counter.

The *burek* was freshly baked. Halid sank his teeth into the crispy dough and remembered how much he had missed the village.

"So, I heard you've come back a rich man," Shukri said as he offered him a bottle of beer. "Here, it's warm. It'll wash the *burek* down nicely. Then you can answer my question."

"Rumors travel faster than a Scud." Halid smiled, savoring the taste.

"Are they rumors?"

Halid didn't answer. Instead he focused on a fly that landed on the edge of the wrapping paper. It was missing a leg.

"Look at it, a cripple, and it's still stealing," he told Shukri, and he crushed the fly with his fingers.

"I see you still have your reflexes," Shukri chuckled.

"My old man taught me to put my hand directly in front of them, and let them fly inside my hand. It's easy once you've learned the trick."

"Do you remember eating a wasp for a bet, back then?" Shukri asked, still smirking.

"Sure."

"Your mouth swelled up so badly. We were afraid your old man was going to kill us if you died."

"I couldn't say a word."

"That wasn't so bad. I bet you won't eat that fly today," Shukri challenged.

"How much?"

"Another bottle."

Halid swallowed the fly. Shukri inspected his hand to make sure he wasn't swindled. They toasted each other. "Zhiveli."

"Have you done any hunting lately?" Shukri asked.

"No. Where? In Sarajevo?"

"Don't get mad. I'm just asking. The dogs have been going wild. There must be the smell of wolf in the air."

"I know. I heard them. But the wolves wouldn't be so close before the snow."

"Did you see your mother?"

Halid emptied his glass. "I don't feel like going home. Or talking about it," he said. "Okay?"

For a moment they sat in silence.

"Can you believe Momir is dead?" Shukri asked.

Halid shook his head.

"A mine. Went to pieces just like that." Shukri snapped his fingers.

"Pretty awful."

"It could've been one of yours."

"It wasn't."

"How can you be sure?"

"I am."

Halid never shared any details of Momir's death with anyone else, afraid of any inappropriate comments and his reaction to them. He secretly visited the site and disabled as many mines as he could, risking court-martial and certain death. For days his only objective had been to discover whether he directly caused Momir's death. He dug feverishly, cloaked in darkness. None of the mines he unearthed bore his platoon's trademark sticker, none.

"I've been meaning to go to his grave, but a Christian graveyard is not a good place for us to be seen. So I help in other ways," Shukri said.

"He was blown to pieces along with two other soldiers," Halid said. "His body was never recovered. What would be the point of going to the grave? He isn't there." Halid circled his finger around the sweating bottle.

"Don't think about it too much." Shukri leaned over the counter and moved the bottle away. "It will muddle your head. They are not our friends anymore. Besides, not one of them is anything like Momir used to be. We have to watch out."

"Watch out? For what?"

"You never know what's bubbling below the surface."

"They've nothing but women left."

"You're right." Shukri smiled. "And some of them are real lookers. Mira for instance."

"What about Mira?" Halid asked. The tone of familiarity and disrespect with which Shukri mentioned her name irked him.

"Calm down. I see you're still sweet on her. After all these years. Well, you should know that the old dragon keeps her on a tight leash."

"How is Stana?"

"Fierce, as always. Just the other day she went after three of our soldiers, fully armed mind you—and not locals. Not somebody who'd spare her. Nobody even knows what for. Looked at her the wrong way, I guess. It took Rade and me some serious negotiating to smooth things over. They were getting ready to throw her in jail."

"At least something's the same."

"Damn right, she bit me when I was trying to hold her

back." He rolled up his sleeve. "Fake teeth hurt like real ones."

They both burst out laughing, and the uneasiness dissipated. Then a second later, as when someone forgets to close the window during bad weather and the high winds whistle through the house, the sadness crept back and Halid stood up to leave.

"I should go," he said.

"We should have a celebration. Go see your mother and come back. I'll go visit the old Gypsy Ghurge at the Korea and see if he'll keep his band going all night. And tomorrow we'll go hunting. Like in the old days."

"I'll go get some money, and I'll meet you in the orchard."

"Go home."

"No."

"Maybe we'll go together later."

"Mother is probably sleeping. She goes to bed early."

"The war has made insomniacs out of all of us," Shukri said. "I'll see you around midnight."

HIS LEGS LIGHTENED FROM THE BEER, HALID WALKED outside into the fresh air. He rubbed his arms with his hands and looked up at the Dinara. The rain had stopped, but the clouds were still gathered low and thick, hiding the peak. He'd been gone for so long he couldn't remember exactly where it stood. He had only climbed it once—the first time he got drunk. That day, Father finagled a bottle of Johnny Walker from a customs official in a card game and woke Halid in the middle of the night. "Come on, boy." He shook Halid until he opened his eyes. "This is a rare opportunity. Let's climb the peak." When they made it about halfway up, they took a break, and Halid had his first few drinks. Father lit a fire and sang patriotic songs. They both got so smashed that Father didn't notice when Halid accidentally peed on his shoe. The next day, well past noon, sick with a hangover, Halid rose to his father reprimanding their dog for ruining his shoes, thinking the poor thing a culprit. When Mother knocked at Halid's bedroom door, Father ordered, "Let him rest, the boy earned it last night."

Father died a year after the war started. In a way, Halid was relieved. Watching the country go mad would've made the old man drink more, which would have been harder on Mother. Two months after the funeral, in one of her letters, Mother complained that the rumors had been buzzing about Father's unsettled gambling debts.

Halid stuck his head back through the tavern door. "Shukri!" he shouted. "When my old man died there were rumors he owed you a lot. Is it true?"

"That's just yapping. But he did owe me a song."

"Which one?"

" 'What Good Is My Life Without You?' "

"Oh, good. That's the only one I know."

"Well, you can pay me back later."

OUT OF CIGARETTES, HE HEADED TOWARD THE GOLDSMITH'S shop on Main Street. The goldsmith's wife, Saliha, a well-known dream interpreter who was once summoned to Sarajevo to help interpret a dream for some influential politician, was also a cigarette dealer. Her husband, Hamdija, was a descendant of many generations of master craftsmen who were famous for their fine work during the Ottoman Empire, back when there was still gold to be bought. Local *beys*, the Muslim landowners, were fond of displaying carefully crafted objects to their guests. Hamdija kept his skill alive by remodeling a single piece of gold he inherited from his forefathers. When he was in a good mood he'd let young Halid hold the precious piece in his hand. Later on, the unlucky man experimented with alloy and mistakenly turned the gold dark brown, which he kept a secret from everyone except Momir and Halid, his trusted favorites. Hamdija was stabbed to death during the first raids. His murderers disappeared empty-handed, leaving an odd-looking auburn metal bird next to the body.

As Halid approached the shop, he saw Saliha sitting outside studying the dark sky.

"Salaam Alekum, Halid," she said, covering her eyebrows with her palm as if shielding her eyes from the sun. "It's good to see you."

"How are you?"

"Alive, but talentless. I can't read people's dreams since my husband died."

"I don't dream anymore," Halid said.

"That's not a bad thing nowadays."

"Got any Marlboros?"

"Sure." She pulled a carton from underneath her skirt and took out a pack.

When Halid offered money, she refused.

"Don't. It's good to be kind to a returning soldier. Maybe I'll get my talent back."

"I hope you do."

"Halid," Saliha yelled behind him, "be careful, please."

"I will." He smiled and waved at her when he realized that the Gypsy boy was following him, failing at being invisible. Halid took longer than necessary to light a cigarette, giving the boy just enough time to come closer. Then he quickly turned around. The boy was no more than ten feet behind him.

"Want one?" he offered.

The boy peered at him suspiciously. His little face was smeared with chocolate, and he was gripping the candy tightly in one hand.

"Are you Halid?" he asked.

"Who wants to know?"

"Isaac Pap."

Finally some good news: Pap was still around.

One of the last Jews in Bosnia, Pap was a friend of the Vejzagic family even before Halid was born. The only elder who was literate, he read the paper to the villagers who came to his house every Saturday night. After he purchased the town's first TV, his living room was always packed with visitors.

Pap's entire family perished during World War II, and he developed a familial relationship with the locals, especially the children. Next to his front door he kept a jar filled with candy, and as long as Halid could remember, he and his friends hung around Pap's kitchen, occasionally stealing from the jar while Pap pretended not to notice. He seldom left his house, except to go to the baths, but he always welcomed guests. On rare occasions he came along on bear hunts with the rest of the men, but he would never touch a gun or help skin the catch. The men called him "tender palms," with affection, and shook their heads in wonder at his closeness to the local women and his insistence on teaching them to read and write, which, for women, was considered a waste of time. "The Jews are different," one of the oldest living Muslims, Akran Pirija, once stated with both authority and understanding. "They forgot the way of the weapons."

Over the years, as Father's attachment to alcohol grew stronger, the bond between Pap and Halid solidified. They spent hours talking. Pap was the only one who knew details about Mira. After he received his draft notice, Halid reported to Pap first. He hid at Pap's during the going-away party Father threw to celebrate the next generation's opportunity to flash its courageous colors. Mother didn't mention

Pap in her letters, and Halid feared that his beloved friend might have succumbed to the horrors of the last four years.

The boy was waiting for his answer.

"Did you get that chocolate as a payment for carrying the message?" Halid asked.

"No, I bought it with the money I got for not selling you the umbrella. Anyway, the old man Pap is at the bathhouse waiting for you, if you are Halid."

"Tell him I'll be over soon."

DURING THE FIVE CENTURIES THEY RULED THE AREA, the Turks lived in a separate part of town, all the way south where the pinewoods started, and rarely mixed with the common Christian folk, the *raja*. Their houses were built on two levels with watchtowers on the top and seven-foot fences designed to keep the unholy Christian eyes from catching glimpses of the harem concubines. The baths were in the center of the Turkish quarters, inside the pasha's old residence. They were never intended for public use but were converted after the emancipation of the serfs. Although the liberated Christians were strongly encouraged to go to the baths, the only people who went were the poor Muslims and the few remaining Sephardim.

Pap's pale body looked small submerged against the turquoise and red mosaics of the pasha's old harem tub that could once fit thirty women.

"Shalom Aleichem, Halid, I heard you were back. Glad to see you in one piece." He offered his clammy hand without getting up.

"Salaam, Pap, how are you?"

"Older."

"I see you're still smoking the Dravas." Halid pointed at the cigarette burning in the ashtray on the tub's edge. The old man had vowed never to smoke an American brand. His younger brother moved to Philadelphia in 1946 and refused to visit, so Pap begrudged anything American.

Halid sat down and took his boots and socks off so he could ease his weary feet in the scalding water.

"It bites today, be careful," Pap warned. "I turned the heater up this morning. It's the only thing that soothes my leg."

Looking more like a deep green silk stocking, the gangrene had spread over Pap's foot and calf, almost all the way up to his knee. Halid didn't want to bring it up; no matter how old and tired a man got, he didn't need to be reminded of dying.

"Gangrene's a bitch," Pap said.

"Does it hurt?"

"Not as much as surgery would."

They both smiled when their eyes met. The old man had made his choice, and although he'd hate losing him, Halid wouldn't dream of interfering.

"Want some *rakija*, Halid? I have a good one, '89."

"I thought it's dangerous for the heart to drink *rakija* when you sit in the bath."

"It is," Pap laughed.

"All right, I'll have one." They toasted silently, sipped, and watched the water gently slosh against the pool walls.

"What do you mean to do now that you're back?" Pap asked.

"I've no idea," Halid whispered.

"It was pretty bad there, wasn't it?"

"Uh-huh."

"Take some time. Get used to being back."

"I've taken three months already."

"That's not much."

"It is when you don't have much to do."

"I know. I come here every day now," Pap said. "It gives me a reason to get out of the house." He splashed hot water over his face and rubbed it with a towel. "Did you see your mother?"

"No, not yet."

"She probably knows you're back already."

"Probably."

"I heard that you came back with a bundle."

"So, everyone knows?"

"I'm not everyone. Did you see Mira yet?"

"No."

"It's not going to be easy, but I can arrange a meeting. I'll see her tonight when I take Mladen home."

Mladen. Halid had completely forgotten about Mladen and hadn't even looked for him at the house. Momir's younger and only sibling, Mladen, known as "a stupid giant," stood well over six feet seven, with his back hunched over and his enormous head hanging down. At the age of nine he was almost six feet tall and did so badly at school that Stana had to keep him home.

"What's he up to?" Halid asked.

"What can he be? He comes here with me and tends to his plants."

Mladen focused all of his attention on the garden and over time became known as a specialist for supersensitive plants. Local kids called Mladen the "botanic man," after the protagonist in a TV series. They borrowed flowering plants from him to impress the stern and scary biology teacher. Nothing could tease a smile out of the old maid's heavily haired upper lip like an African lily could. Fortunately the lily was Mladen's favorite and grew abundantly in his garden.

For years the town's wise men sanctioned the bond between Mladen and the children. But all of that changed when a girl's body washed up on the river's edge. Her neck had been snapped with one clean twist—the work of someone endowed with enormous strength: a giant. All clues pointed to Mladen. If he hadn't been Momir's brother, and if Momir hadn't been the best center the soccer team ever had, the investigation would have gone further, possibly to trial. But for centuries, matters were settled differently around here. Honorably and among men. The real court, not the court of big-city lawyers and judges, but the dozen *beys* and *hajji* who met every night at the bench by the river and arbitrated on important matters, expected Momir to settle the incident with the girl's family.

"How's the town treated him since Momir died?"

"How should they? As always. All that was long ago."

The girl was poor and survived by only a grand-aunt. She could make better use of a new means of transportation and a few more trinkets than the trouble a trial would bring. As a young neighbor drove the weeping grand-aunt to church in a new carriage dragged by a new mule, the village looked on. Her mourning shoulders were wrapped in a hand-knit shawl—a contribution from Stana. The real court ruled the dispute resolved.

Still fearing formal government intervention, Stana forbade Mladen from wandering around town. She asked Momir and Halid to build a cage for him in the middle of the yard to keep him locked up while everyone was in the fields. "We'll make it beautiful," she promised. "No one will be able to say the Milosnic family kept their own worse than the government would. Let them send their city snoopers around here, we have nothing to hide."

When Momir and Halid's artistry proved to be worth "as much as the last year's snow," Stana dragged the best pieces of furniture into the cage.

"So? Do you want to see Mira or not?" Pap asked.

"I guess I'll have to. Sooner or later."

"You were never a good liar," Pap said as he tried to pull a sock back on his swollen foot.

"Sometimes I was."

"Not really. Anyway, I'll send you word by tomorrow." Pap smiled. "By my little Gypsy devil."

"You and your collection of misfits," Halid replied. "Where did this one come from?"

"One of Ghurge's."

"I heard from Shukri he's still around. I thought that he'd be the first one to take off when the army retreated. How many kids has he got now?"

"You can count them tonight. I hear Shukri means to welcome you home at the Korea."

THE NORTHERN WIND BLEW THROUGH THE BATHHOUSE corridor. The empty sleeves of the shirts hanging on the clothesline stood upright.

"Hey Halid," Mladen yelled, pointing at the shirts, smiling with his tremendous lips. "You know what this means. There'll be a lot of dead soldiers in the air tonight. Leave an extra plate at your dinner table for the hungry ghosts."

Halid shivered. The distorted features on Mladen's oversized face somehow still reminded him of Momir.

"Halid, say hello to your mother," Mladen continued. "Ask her to bake me one of her pies."

Halid waved his arm. "You say hello to Stana for me."

"I can't. We're not allowed to mention any of you anymore."

Halid smiled. Mladen always told the truth.

"Don't forget the pies. Any kind is fine. Cranberries, blueberries, even cheese pie." Mladen followed Halid to the gate. "Meat too! Meat pie would be great."

Tucking his face into his turtleneck, Halid hurried back to the orchard, hoping to build a fire unnoticed and warm himself before he headed to the Korea at night. He would think about going home later—much later.

Back in the yard, he retrieved his suitcase from behind the rosebush and removed a wad of bills. They were cold and damp, reminding him of how chilly the mountain nights were. Yet it was too late to wake Mother seeking shelter from the cold. He couldn't sleep in the barn: it would upset the dogs. With the help of a flashlight he found his favorite tree in their plum orchard and sat beneath it. The autumn grass had begun to yellow and harden. He lit a cigarette, picked a plum up from the ground, and split it in half. His match was still burning and he saw that the plum was red and orange on the inside, without any worms. Good, he thought, closing his eyes.

3

MIRA CLIMBED INTO BED AT TEN O'CLOCK.
The day had been full of Stana's fussing and snarls, and although she was too agitated to fall asleep, her room was her only sanctuary. She left the lights on and listened to the bugs batting against the bedroom walls. She hated the bugs. They would stay away if the lights were off, but darkness made everything worse. The quiet quieter, the loud louder.

A thick moth smashed into the bulb, and it flickered. Don't go out. Don't go out, she pleaded. Damn bugs, making a mess. She could close the window. But the midday heat still lingered in her room. The cooler night air kept her son comfortable and asleep, giving her some rest.

Mira occupied the smallest room in the house. After Momir died, Stana had Mira and her four-year-old son, Ivan, move all of their belongings into a small cubicle above the kitchen with space enough for only a single bed and one trunk. Stana blamed Mira for all of their family's calamities. As Mira set up the bed she was to share with her son, Stana lifted the top of the trunk and scoffed, "You jinx, pack what you own in here. It's small enough to fit the puny dowry you brought to this house."

Somebody pounded at the front door and yelled, "Anybody home?"

Mira tensed. Who could it be? She should answer. Her bedroom was closest to the entrance. Clutching the curtain, she peeked through her bedroom window and recognized the round, bald head shining under the front-door bulb: it was Rade, the baker. What the devil could he want at this hour? she wondered.

Rade knocked again, this time louder, and shouted, "Is there anybody home?"

"Coming," she whispered, scared that he would rouse not only her son but Stana too. She'd certainly blame all of this commotion on Mira. Wrapping a bedcover around her shoulders, she ran toward the door.

"Coming," she said louder.

When she opened the door to Rade's face, plump as always, red and shiny, she noticed two burlap bags in a small wheelbarrow. Mira sized him up. She had never trusted him. His eyes were too small, too close to his nose. His skin was hairless, leathery, and dimply, like that of a peasant woman. Worst of all, he gave Muslim names to his children and received all sorts of privileges in return: the pastures close to the water, a brother-in-law running the mill, clothes for his kids during shortages. She knew that he cheated everyone, especially the poor. When Stana forced her to socialize with his family, Mira would wipe her hands on her apron and spit against bad luck every time she touched something he had held. Maybe others respected that he kept to himself and never bothered anyone, but she was convinced that there was as much good in him as there were legs on a snake.

"I brought you some flour," Rade said. "Take it inside."

"Flour? What for? We didn't ask."

"I went over my bills. I saw I made a mistake, so I'm paying you back."

The two bags looked to be fifty pounds each. Some mistake, she thought. How was that possible? She didn't remember giving the baker a *dinar*.

"Did you borrow money from the old lady, and I don't know about it?" she asked.

"No, I just caught it in my books. I owed you a hundred pounds, so I'm paying you fair and square."

"I can't take this. You'll come back and say you made another mistake, and we'll have to pay you."

"Listen, all I'm saying is that I have to give you this, and you can take it or leave it here to rot for all I care."

"Take or leave what? What's she got to take or leave?" Stana appeared, her hair disheveled, her black housedress unbuttoned. Once a teenager of reputed beauty, Stana got fat with her first son, hunched over in the middle of her back with her second, and developed a cluster of moles around her mouth with her last, a stillborn. The change was so drastic that it shamed the house, and her husband refused to be seen with her in public. When they were invited to weddings or funerals he made her cover her face with a veil. After he died, she wore it to his funeral. From then on, she wore nothing but the black housedress—she even slept in it.

"She's got no business taking or leaving a thing in this house."

"Salaam, Stana, I sure am glad to see you. This thing here"—he pointed at Mira—"she won't let me do my business, and I came out here in the middle of the night."

"Can't you do anything right?" Stana barked at Mira. "What did you do this time?"

"I came to drop off this flour I owe you—two bags. I owed you seventy-five pounds from before, but I added twenty-five so you people wouldn't say, 'the baker doesn't pay his debts.' And this good-for-nothing girl didn't even ask me inside."

Mira was boiling mad. As the widow of a man who fought for the losing side, she meant nothing around here. At least her husband fought and didn't hide behind some excuses, like this thick-skinned bastard with his Muslim-named litter. Oh, he just couldn't leave his young children. She wished she could slap him across his cowhide of a face and tell him that his eyes shrank because he spent too much time going over numbers, making sure nobody took a penny more than they ought to. The blubbery coward had a lot of nerve calling her good-for-nothing.

"My goodness, the way you are all carrying on, one would think it's broad daylight." A voice came from down the road. Mira recognized it: Pap. He and Mladen emerged from behind the lavender bush—Pap was approaching with his arms open, while Mladen trailed behind.

"So," he asked, "what are you all doing here?"

Mira was glad to see Pap. He'd shut up the old lady. His news reading and radio listening intimidated Stana, and she toned down her ranting at Mira when he was around. Rade too would have to retreat.

"Go to bed, Mladen. Let us do our business," Stana said. Mladen squeezed between the two women. Mira stepped back to let him pass and smiled at him discreetly. The old lady hated that the two got along. They all stood in silence until they heard Mladen pull the heavy cage door closed behind him.

"Rade has something to give back to us, and your favorite fool here is making a mess of it," Stana said to Pap, pointing at Mira.

"What is it that can't wait till daylight?" Pap asked.

"Seems that Rade owed us some flour."

"Yes." Rade avoided Pap's eyes. "I owed you seventy-five pounds, maybe a few more, but I brought two bags, a hundred pounds to pay you back... to be fair."

"How Christian of you," Pap said.

"I just did my books," Rade said, backing away to his cart. "Take the bags or leave them."

"Oh, they'll take them. Now, can we all go inside? My leg is killing me," he said while taking his shoes off.

"Here, she can carry them, I need to get home." Rade dumped the two bags at their doorstep.

It was past midnight, Mira realized, and she decided to leave the cursed bags outside the house. She knew that Pap wouldn't make such a late call if he didn't have something important to tell her. Not this late. The road was deserted, and he usually let Mladen walk home on his own. Another secret they kept from Stana: for months now she and Pap had been trying to teach Mladen to be more independent. She followed Pap as a great unease settled over her.

"Stana," Pap said. "Do you mind if Mira tends to my leg? It's been throbbing all day."

"Suit yourself. I'm going back to my hammock."

The house was quiet again. Relieved that Stana was gone, Mira rushed to the kitchen to start the fire. Earlier that evening she had prepared the kettle with water and a bunch of dried chamomile for a soothing potion. An hour after dinner, when Pap hadn't shown up yet, she gave up on waiting and put everything away. She'd have to do it again. The chair creaked loudly under Pap's weight, and Mira clumsily clattered the kettle, almost pouring its contents over the fire.

"I've warned you things were falling apart around here," he said.

She couldn't stand the suspense anymore.

"Tell me what's wrong," she said. "I know that something's wrong."

"Halid is back."

Mira squeezed the handle on the kettle. Pap was an old friend—had always been. He brought the news that her husband had been blown to pieces. Stana knew for hours before, but she wouldn't tell Mira. Pap stayed up with her that night. But he was also a man. She kept her face then, she was not going to lose it now.

"Let's see your leg," she said.

The stain had widened during the last few months. Mira knew Pap was not going to be around much longer. Stana once mentioned there might be some hope if an operation was performed. She even asked Mira to try to influence Pap. Partly because she was leery of doctors, and partly because she didn't want to do anything that would please the old lady, but mostly because she wanted to leave the sick man in peace, Mira refused. Now, while she was bathing his leg in the tea water, scrubbing it as hard as he could bear, she would much rather discuss doctors than Halid.

"There," Mira said. "Step on the towel." She carefully

dabbed the leg and gently rolled his cuff back down. "Your foot is a little swollen, so don't tie your laces too tightly." She avoided looking at him; he'd know what she was thinking. Pap tried to stand up but stumbled.

"Hot water," he said, "makes the blood flow, but it hurts." He grabbed a chair.

"Here." Mira offered her shoulder.

They inched toward the front door, pausing twice for Pap to catch his breath.

"You know," Mira said, "maybe surgery would help."

"He's in the orchard waiting to see you."

"Maybe I don't want to see him."

"I think you should."

"I can walk you home if you want."

"No, I'll be okay. Listen, he's come back with a bundle."

"What does that have to do with me?"

"I don't want you to end up alone in this house."

"I am not alone."

"With me gone? You will be."

"Don't," she said, trying to hush him.

"All I'm suggesting is that you see what he has to say."

"What is the matter with you, Pap? Have you forgotten what he's like? He'll have a million things to say, and he'll do none of them."

Pap let go of Mira's shoulder. He turned to face her. She knew he meant well and that he worried about her, but she would not be told what to do.

"What are you going to do when I die?"

"I'll go to Serbia and get a job."

"With a four-year-old and no schooling? Doing what? You'll not only ruin yourself, you'll ruin the boy. You have no right to do that."

Mira was sure that Pap hadn't intended to insult her, but he had done so just the same. It was time for him to go.

"Good night," she said.

"I'm sorry."

"That's okay. You still don't want me to help you to your house?"

"No. I'll be fine."

"Then be careful on your way. All that rain tore up the road. There are potholes everywhere."

"Mira, I'm sorry for what I said."

"I know you are. Go now."

MIRA STARED DOWN THE ROAD LONG AFTER PAP HOBBLED into the darkness. The air was heavy. She realized she was barefoot in the caked mud and she'd have to wipe her feet before she climbed back into bed. The bags sat where Rade had left them. The mud couldn't be good for the flour. She thought of the wet towel on the floor and reminded herself to pick it up. By morning it would start to mildew. The rest of the kitchen needed tidying too. She hooked the towel above the stove, emptied the teapot, rinsed it, hung it up to dry, and checked the milk buckets inside the stove to see if they needed mixing. It wouldn't help a bit if the milk went sour.

She would pick a few tomatoes for tomorrow. Maybe there would be an egg by the morning. She must remember to check the henhouse. With some fresh tomatoes and a scrambled egg or two she could feed a whole house. If Stana wanted to use Rade's flour later and bake the bread, let her. She wouldn't touch it for the world.

She rearranged the kindling and lowered the fire on the stove, then changed her mind and added a log. Just in case, she thought as she headed toward the garden. We need good milk around here.

The light above the door leading into the garden had been out since before the bombing. Mladen was sleeping with his mouth open like a child. Trusting, she thought, I was trusting once. And beautiful. Her throat was tight. She squeezed the cage bars with her hands and pushed her face into her knuckles.

"Damn you," she whispered, as tears came. "Damn you." Mladen opened his eyes.

"Is it breakfast time?" he asked.

"No, not yet," she said. "Go back to sleep."

"Lock the door, please," Mladen said. "I don't want anyone sneaking in while I'm sleeping."

"Sure, sweetheart, good night."

Mladen closed his eyes and turned over. Mira locked the

padlock, wiped her face, and spat the salty taste from her mouth.

"Damn you," she repeated. Of all the people who left, he was the last one she expected to reappear. He always wanted more, she knew, more than these mountains and a wasted woman could offer. "A thinker," her cousin said about him once. "It's a curse for a man to be so preoccupied with his own mind."

As she stepped outside the front door, she looked toward Halid's house. The light was on in one of the windows and a small shadow quickly pulled away. Then it went out. Poor woman, Mira thought. He hasn't been home yet. She wasn't the only one he was tormenting.

She knew that Stana was in the hammock, listening. Not a sound would be missed. Stana hadn't really slept since the war and had the hammock lashed to the window frame so she could watch the road. Mira didn't care. Let Stana feast her eyes. Mira had always been her favorite spectacle. The orchard was the only thing on her mind.

4

THE ROAD WAS DARKER THAN SHE

expected—pitch-black, without a single star. Strange, she
thought, trying to avoid potholes, Halid could have walked
up and down this road today. Right now, she could be step-
ping inside his footsteps without knowing. Somewhere under
all this dirt there could be each of Halid's footprints to and
from his village since before the war. Eager on the way out,
and certain, heels deep in the ground from marching. Then,
reluctant, dragging his feet on the way back.

A familiar figure slouched over a fire's last embers with a red cigarette tip glowing near the face. So, she thought, he finally gave in to smoking. She wondered what he looked like. Nervous, she checked the buttons on her dress and straightened her scarf over her forehead. What should she say? She didn't know. Let him do the talking. He had asked to see her first. Not too much, because he was smooth with words. He could convince her of anything. No matter what he said, she should not get too close. Be smart, keep your distance, don't look at his eyes, not for long. Unlike most men who had either women or money on their minds, Halid was different. His mind was full of many things, mostly of trouble.

The cigarette tip lit up as he inhaled. She saw new lines above his eyebrows. He looked so thin.

She leaned against a young plum tree and watched him smoke. His hand moved slowly but firmly toward his face. His shoulders almost touched his ears. He was obviously thinking about something upsetting. Or someone. This was new to her. She used to know everything there was to know about Halid. Always quiet, gentle, and comforting, he was not his father's son—no shortness of temper, no cross words. He leaned over to stub out his cigarette. Her stomach knotted. That was how he leaned over her, the first time they were alone, and gave her the hair clip. She was sixteen, and happy. Later that night, her clothes all wrinkled and dusty, she sat at the table for dinner and couldn't stop smiling. Too excited to eat, she excused herself and ran into the bedroom she shared with three sisters and two female cousins to try on her present.

She exhaled trying to keep quiet. She remembered the milk on the stove and regretted adding that last log. If she hadn't, she would have had a perfect reason to return to the house quickly.

"Pap said you were back," she whispered.

"It's been a long time," he said without turning.

Then he rose, faced her, and offered his hand. It seemed silly to shake hands with Halid, but she responded. His grip was firm and warm. "You are very thin," she said.

"There wasn't much to eat in the trenches."

"I thought there was always plenty for the soldiers."

"Not always."

They stood with their hands locked. Then he offered her a cigarette and lit one for himself. She accepted.

"How long have you been back?"

"A day."

"I heard you were shot."

"It's healing."

"How come you returned? I didn't think you would."

"There was no more room in the hospital. They asked me to leave."

That hurt, and she was angry that it did. She knew better than to expect he would ever say he came back because of her. She even anticipated that he would disappear, like he did the week she was told the marriage had been arranged between her and Momir and she asked to see him.

"So you came back because you had nowhere else to go?" she asked. "It's a good thing nobody was waiting for you."

He took a drag. He was hurt now, she knew, but she didn't care. If he came for nothing, he was getting nothing.

"Is anybody else coming back?" she asked.

"No. Nothing around here to come back to."

"Well, we had a war around here too."

"I know."

"So what do you plan to do now that you're back? Do you plan to work your father's land?" she asked.

"I don't know," he said. "I'm too tired to talk about that right now. I'm too tired for talking about anything."

"Then why did you ask to see me?"

"Pap said I should."

"You mean to tell me that this was all Pap's idea? That I'm here because he suggested it?"

"Mira, please, don't get upset. Sit next to me, please."

She picked a tree far enough away from him to feel safe and sat down. Halid took the flashlight out of the suitcase and sat next to her. She prayed that he would not turn it on. She hadn't seen her own reflection in a while.

"Oh, don't turn that thing on, we can see," she said. "Besides, the moon should be out any minute."

He didn't respond.

He took her hand and placed his face inside her palm. His beard scratched her, and she could smell him. It was a different smell, unclean. Halid was dirty.

"Halid, no." She wriggled her hand away from his face. "I should be getting home. It's late."

"Please, Mira, listen. I did the best I could. There was nothing I could have done, the war was starting."

"What are you talking about?" she asked, getting up. "Are you drunk?"

"I'm sorry I left the way I did."

"I was already married, remember? You ran away like a little boy, weeks before the war."

"A week. All I had was a week. You can't blame me for not being able to do the right thing in a week."

"It doesn't take a week to do the right thing. Why are we even talking about this? It's the past, Halid."

"Listen to me," he started. "Maybe we can make it work this time."

"You were never one to say stupid things, Halid, so don't start now. Look!" She grabbed the flashlight, switched it on, and pulled her scarf off. "My hair fell out. I had typhoid fever. Nothing to eat for four years." He turned his head away.

"Here." She opened her mouth. "I lost half my teeth too. And you? You got Marlboros."

Halid reached his arms out and tried to hug her. She looked at him astonished and pushed him away.

"You think that's what I want?"

He dropped his head in shame. "I'm sorry for your troubles, so sorry. I wish I knew what to do. I want to make it better now."

"How?"

"Maybe I can help take care of the kid."

"Nobody is taking care of my son but me."

"How is he?"

"None of your business."

"Mira, please."

"Growing."

"That's good."

"Growing into nothing. He has less than I had growing up."

"Mira, I brought some money with me."

"What does that have to do with me?"

"Maybe we could go away."

"You know damn well that the old woman would never let me leave town with my son."

"I can offer her money."

"You mean, buy him?"

"Not him. Stana was always for sale."

"Not since Momir died."

"I could offer her a tractor."

"You have enough for a tractor?" She didn't know of anyone who had that much money, not even the oil smugglers. "Where did you get that much?"

"Some from the government. Some from some deals. If you'll let me, I'll come and talk to Stana in the morning."

She looked at him, perplexed, not sure what to make of his talk. Getting away from Stana's ever-growing rancor was tempting. Halid took her hand in his.

"I missed you," he whispered and kissed it.

She looked at him blankly and said, "You know what I missed? I missed knowing where the next meal was coming from. Don't think that everybody around here is for sale."

"I'm sorry."

"You have nothing to be sorry about. You should take that money and spend it on yourself. Go, have fun."

"Mira, the war can change a man. I'm different too. Not a spender. Honest. I sent you the flour, didn't I?"

"What?" She was surprised at first.

Then she started to laugh, quietly at first, covering her mouth with her hand, but then she let go. She didn't care if he could see the bare gums where her pretty teeth used to be.

"Of course, it was you! I knew I was right. I have never been wrong about a man. Not a man like Rade." She tossed her head back with new vigor, feeling better. "Rade, miss a hundred pounds of flour? Never. I have to go now." She stood up. "But welcome back. I hope you find something here that will make your coming worthwhile."

"I'll be by tomorrow to talk with Stana."

"Suit yourself. You know she won't talk to you. You'll be lucky to keep your head on your shoulders."

ON HER WAY BACK FROM THE ORCHARD SHE WANTED TO run. The nerve of that man: to come back and think they could repeat the past. The naïve girl who waited for him in a hunting shack in the woods for three days was no more. She had sent the message that she needed to see him, and for three days that silly child sat by herself in the dark, too scared to light even a candle, afraid she'd be found out. Finally, at the dawn of the fourth day, a boy arrived carrying a message from Halid's mother: it said her son had gone hunting, have a happy marriage. That evening, when it was dark enough to cover her shame, she snuck back into her house, her face swollen with tears, and surrendered, half-conscious, to her mother's and aunts' hands for dressing. One woman was sent to town to bring ice to take care of the puffiness. She and Momir were married the next morning.

Then she heard a rustle in the corn. She wasn't sure if it was getting closer or moving farther away. She listened. It sounded like panting. Maybe it was just a breeze, she thought. Still, she picked up the pace. When she got close to the house she found Stana standing outside the door, tugging on one of the bags.

"I don't want all this flour to go bad," she said. "Where the hell have you been?"

"I walked Pap home," Mira lied. If she told Stana the truth, she'd be turned out of the house in a minute. "His leg hurt, and there are all those potholes everywhere. I wanted to make sure he didn't fall."

"That old fool. Walking in this bad weather, just so you can wash his foot. Anyway, help me with these bags. They won't be of use to anyone if the flour rots."

The burlap scraped Mira's skin, and she let the bag drop. "It's too heavy."

"What's the matter, princess, a little burlap too rough for your delicate hands?"

"It's too heavy. I'll go get Mladen."

"Don't you disturb my son," Stana yelled at her. "He's sleeping. If you can't do it, I'll do it myself. You go back to your room, or go check on your son, you good-for-nothing mother."

Mira was too worn out to fight with Stana. Better to do something else, keep herself busy. In two hours the colicky cow had to be milked. The poor thing had broken through the fence into a field of fresh hay and now she was bursting with gas. Mira had walked her around the barn all afternoon, and she was able to pass some manure and ease herself, but if they were to keep her alive and wet teated, she had to be milked tonight. It wouldn't hurt if she did it now, and then again a few hours later. Any work was better than lying awake in bed.

In the barn, Mira squeezed a hardened teat and a stream of foul-smelling milk trickled out. She was nauseated. Why was he back? It wasn't like him to return. The cow mooed and shuffled. "Steady, girl, steady." Mira rubbed the bloated belly and placed her forehead on the warm hind. Why doesn't he just go away?

Then she heard a commotion from the house. Stana was in the hallway, calling her name. Her son was up. Fine, she thought, she'd give him a bath. Mira tiptoed into the boy's room and found him sound asleep. The old woman, she'd scheme to no end just to upset me, she thought. He probably didn't even make a peep. Still, she should wash him. He was ripe for cleaning, and he fought it when he was awake, saying he could do it himself. Already ashamed to be sponged by a woman.

She dragged a half-filled tub upstairs. She pulled his pajamas off—not a flinch. He'd grown so big, she could hardly lift him up. The boy's head, long and narrow like his father's, was tilted back on his pillow, leaning to the left slightly. He almost always slept in that position. He had grown so much this summer. He'd be five soon, starting school. Her back was sore. Exhausted, she covered him with his pajamas, knelt on the floor by his bed, and rested her head on the mattress. She could smell the cow's hind on her face. Her boy would be a grown man soon. Old enough to fight. The water in the tub had stopped sloshing. She could hear a bug buzzing through the air. What would happen tomorrow? She was too drained even for worry.

5

THE WIND ABATED RIGHT AFTER MIRA LEFT, and the dogs had quieted down for the night. The ashes in the fire had cooled. There were no stars, and the moon was white and dim. At least it would be warmer tomorrow, Halid thought. If the dogs were asleep, the wolves must have gone farther up the mountain. They stayed in the higher altitudes during warm weather. His arm was not hurting. That was a good weather predictor as well.

Mira's harshness surprised him. The war had calloused

her. While he was in the trenches he often thought of her, trying to predict what she would say when she first saw him. He remembered her with her hair down, her skirt slightly over the knee, smiling. He had hoped she would forgive him.

It was almost midnight and Shukri would be by soon. The sweat and the smell from the day on the bus lingered and he decided to wash in the stream. The water would be icy, but how could he show up reeking after winning the war? He folded his jacket and pants on top of his boots. Then he hid his Luger and the belt in the bushes by the edge of the stream.

The water pushed against the clay banks. The temperature was close to freezing. This would be a quick bath. He tried to sink his toes into the clay for balance, but it was solid. He pushed harder. Nothing. Drawing a deep breath, he dove, bracing himself for the cold. As he hit the water his chest almost burst. "Yoy," he screamed as he came back to the surface. His chin and cheeks were on fire. He dunked his face back under and opened his eyes to nothing but the dull color of mud.

This was once a fishing haven, best known for trout and pike. Trout. He laughed to himself. As if he knew anything about trout. The damn fish proved too smart for his bottomless metal barrels, the only fishing tools he could ever afford. In vain, young Halid jammed the barrel over the thickest reeds and stirred its contents with his leg, hoping to brush against the cold scales of a trout. He should have known better than to try to catch a trout without a rod. The best he ever did was old catfish.

He pulled himself out of the water, shaking, but with a clearer mind. Solving his problems with Mira and Stana would have to wait until later. The moon had brightened and he could see beyond the stream. The land on the other side belonged to his uncles. There, underneath the third row of corn, lay his family's stash of weapons. In '91, right before the war, he and his cousins used to practice shooting in that field. It was far enough from the police station. Back then, the water was so polluted by the chemical factory that they had to cross the stream wearing rubber fishing boots that reached to their waists. Otherwise they'd get skin rashes. The fish had been gone for more than five years.

Shukri arrived. "Halid, you've gone nuts. It's freezing in there."

"You're going to get yourself killed, sneaking about like that," Halid replied. "Lucky I left my Luger on my belt."

"What else were you going to do? Dive in with it? If you're so worried about safety, why did you dive into the Zabljak?" Shukri was laughing. "Be serious. You still carry that old Luger?"

"Sure, are you kidding? The guns they gave us were shit. You couldn't hit an ox from ten feet."

"How's the water? Cold?"

"Clean. If the war was good for anything, it was good for shutting Yugo-Petrol down."

"Do you think we'll ever get the fish back?" Shukri asked.

"We might get some. Probably not trout."

"You and your trout. We have all this fun ahead of us and

you're standing here mourning over some fish. Do you know anyone who ever caught trout here?"

"Nope."

"I didn't think so. It's a goddamn myth, like the rest of the stories . . . except, I hope, the one about your money. That one is true, right?"

"You're yapping like a woman. Don't worry. There'll be plenty of food and drink for you tonight."

"And women! Women! I could have stayed home if I wanted food."

"All right, all right." Halid laughed.

"Get dressed. Somebody may walk by and get the wrong idea."

"What, that you don't like women?" Halid said as he was drying. He took a wad of bills out of his pocket and offered three from the top to Shukri.

"What's that?"

"For you."

"Oh, come on," Shukri objected.

"It's for you."

"Are you sure? You know I can entertain myself cheaply."

"I'm sure."

"Thanks."

By the time Halid was dressed the moon was dark again and they had to stick by the orchard fence to get back to the main road. Halid wondered if Shukri knew he had seen Pap.

"Did Mira come to see you yet?" Shukri asked.

"Yeah. She's mad at me."

"That's hardly news. What did she have to say?"

That's just how things were around here: everybody's nose in your soup. So you better make sure you have no strange noodles.

"Not much."

"Did she talk about the kid?"

Now he wanted to smack Shukri.

"She didn't want to talk about anything. She's different. Bitter. Because of war and Momir, maybe."

"Well, I don't blame her for hating you. You were never all that good-looking." They looked at each other and Shukri burst out laughing.

"God, I need a drink," Halid said.

"We're on our way, man, on our way."

6

THE KOREA WAS AN OLD GYPSY COLONY ON
the north side of town. The land had belonged to the cotton
factory, which was insolvent almost from the moment it
opened in the late fifties. The cotton grew four hundred
miles away in Macedonia and needed to be transported by a
railroad, which was never finished, and the town's only road
couldn't accommodate heavy trucks. Eventually workers
were laid off and had to collect government support. A de-
cree was passed and the factory was shut down.

The army oversaw the plant's closing and prevented riots. The production buildings were locked up and fenced in barbed wire and the barracks were emptied out. The day the army tanks left town, the Gypsies moved into the barracks. That night they threw the biggest *dernek* celebration the Korea had ever seen, to commemorate the first permanent roof over the *Cigans'* heads. The local police allowed them to stay, as long as the crime and prostitution were kept under cover. The mud around the Korea was always at least three inches deep. Halid shied away from what they called night raids, which were the late-night visits to the girls. He was too embarrassed to come only for music and be labeled less than a man.

As Halid and Shukri arrived, a crowd of children, older women, and young men gathered around them. The younger girls of not over ten, copper colored as the fire around which they gathered, circled an old Gypsy woman with a black baking pan in her hands, the favorite fortune-telling tool. The woman crossed herself before she twirled the pan on one side. The longer she could keep the pan from falling, the better the luck for the person who asked the question. It was strange to see a Gypsy cross herself. Those who sold cheese and meat to his mother were Muslim.

Shukri asked for Ghurge, the community patriarch. A stout man of probably fifty—Gypsies never recorded births—Ghurge occupied the biggest barrack. He was not a full-blooded Gypsy. His father was a Serb, "an influential man from the capital," as Ghurge referred to him. He had cut his father's face from a picture and glued it onto the portrait of Tito left in one of the meeting rooms after the party members evacuated. President Tito was proudly saluting in his snow-white marshal's uniform. Ghurge's father's face fit perfectly. "My marshal," he said in tears when they hung it on the wall.

Ghurge's band, "the Orchestra," was famous throughout three counties. His eighteen children and twenty siblings all played either guitars, violins, or harmonicas. There wasn't a song they couldn't play.

Ghurge had been married four times, but he had chased away the first three wives, and finally married a young girl of ten or eleven. The marriage caused tension in the family. The issue was not her age; matches like this were common in the area. The problem was religion. She was Muslim. He was Christian Orthodox. As the procession led the new bride through town, Ghurge's outraged daughters lay flat across the road and refused to get up until their new mother was properly baptized. The local priest refused to perform the conversion, threatening to shoot everyone. The girl's parents refused to take her back. Then a miracle happened: with tears in her eyes the girl sang a sad song of an unloved bride in the most beautiful voice Ghurge had ever heard. He swore that he would never let an angel like that slip through his fingers. Immediately she was welcomed as an addition to the family, and inaugurated as the band's lead singer.

Halid regretted coming. He had never liked Ghurge—his

shady business, the perpetual mud. All he wanted was to snatch a bottle and leave, but there was little chance of that.

Ghurge was sitting on a white leather sofa outside his barrack surrounded by bright silk pillows. Everything was speckled with bits of mud. Two color television sets behind him played the same music channel. The picture of Ghurge's father in the snow-white uniform sat on one of the televisions. Ghurge had two of his older sons greet the visitors with bread and salt. Halid took only bread, no salt.

"We're here for some fun," Shukri said.

"It will cost you." Ghurge grinned. "Things are different around here."

"Halid came back with a bundle."

"How big?"

"Big enough. He gave your son ten marks."

"Ten! To my son? Which one?"

"The little one. The one that's always in town."

"Oh, the tone-deaf little thief. Lale!" he yelled. "Laaaale! Get over here."

The small head popped through the door. "What do you want?" the boy asked.

"Where are my ten marks?"

"What ten marks, are you drunk?"

"Don't make me get up. The ten Halid gave you."

"He gave me nothing."

"You're lucky I'm in a good mood now, or I'd beat your ass. But I may change my mind later. Go tell your stepmother and your sisters that we have customers. If you want"—he turned to Halid and Shukri—"I could show you some of the imported goods I have for sale."

"Sure."

"Come this way."

Ghurge led them to a rectangular cement building behind his barrack. He unlocked the metal door.

"Are we safe here?" Shukri asked, looking at the "High Voltage" sign affixed to the door.

"Don't worry, I hung that sign to keep my kids away. But it is a fortress. Look here." He pointed to bullet marks all over the door. "One of my brothers, the one I don't speak to, tried to rob me while I was gone."

Inside the square windowless room were five six-foot stashes of cigarette cartons, a dozen five-gallon canisters of gasoline, hanging strips of dried meat and military coats, old musical instruments, and boxes of gloves and socks. On top of an old-fashioned Singer sewing machine there were several brand-new rifles and a revolver.

"I've got what you want," Ghurge said. "And if I don't, I can get it."

Halid had heard smugglers could get their hands on almost anything. Since the war started there were more goods on the black market than ever, but the brand-new AK-97s? Those couldn't be over six months old.

"Do you have any Marlboros?" Shukri asked.

"No. Pap's on good terms with the commissioner, and he told me he'd close me down if I sold American."

"Where did the AK-97s come from?" Halid asked.

"That I couldn't tell you. Are you interested?"

"No."

"We really came here for the music," Shukri said. "Halid just got back today. Maybe we could talk business later."

"Well, you should have said that from the beginning," Ghurge said. He noticed Halid staring at the weapons. "This is not the only fortress around here. My sons all have good guns and know how to use them."

"Is that supposed to scare us?" Halid asked.

Then, his voice softening, Ghurge said, "I don't mean to sound unfriendly. But you both know how much things have changed around here. And for the worse. One can never be too careful."

THE BAND HAD ALREADY ASSEMBLED WHEN HALID AND Shukri sat down and ordered drinks. Then Ghurge's singer wife came out. A necklace of gold coins covered her flat chest. Her face was round and pretty. She smiled and took the tambourine. Behind her, the music started. Halid did not recognize the song.

Ghurge brought the drinks himself and slapped Halid on the shoulder.

"So what did you think about those cigarettes? Rothmans. Not American, I know, but not local either."

"I'll think about it," Halid said, uninterested.

"Of all the people I thought would come home rich . . ."

Ghurge said, leaning toward Halid. "Well, glad you're back. Cheers."

Ghurge stank of *rakija*. The stench was more than a few days old. Halid hated men who stayed drunk. They made terrible soldiers, bad shots, and they fell asleep during watch. They volunteered more than the "dry boys," but they got killed twice as much. *Rakija* makes a lion out of a man first, then it makes an ass. He finished his drink without toasting.

"Look at her." Ghurge pointed to his wife. "Golden. If only I could get her to sing every day, but she has to go to school. I'd have to marry her for real, town hall and everything, to keep her home, but the judge says not until she's sixteen. All I need is for someone to come along and steal her and then my orchestra will be ruined."

"Do you have any others?" Shukri grinned. "Maybe not so talented for singing, but for other things?"

"You'll have to ask my son Milo," Ghurge replied, indignant. "I am a sensitive man, a musician, and I don't meddle in matters of the flesh."

His words annoyed Halid. Halid took his Luger out and placed it quietly on the table. "I see your tongue is wet already, Ghurge. You've had too many. That's always a bad sign."

"Me and my kids are here to please you." Ghurge bowed down, keeping his eyes on the gun. "Dika," he yelled, "give the hero another shot. And send Milo over."

Milo used to run his "business" at night from the rear counter at the bus station outside the Korea. The station was a gathering point for pilgrims going to Sinj Madonna. Thousands of Catholics would flock together before beginning their forty-mile walk over the harshest parts of the Dinara. It was particularly crowded during the summer months. At that time of year business flourished, and Milo had his older brother bring him several girls back from Germany and Italy as reinforcements for their small group. Halid wondered how Milo could continue to conduct business now that the police patrolled the station twenty-four hours a day.

Milo appeared with a cigarette in his mouth, wearing a pink silk shirt. Halid remembered seeing the same shirt years before.

"Nice color," Shukri laughed.

"Ghurge said you wanted to see me?" Milo wasn't amused.

"Yeah. My friend here is back from the war, and we were wondering if you had anything special to celebrate his homecoming."

"How special?"

"How much is very special?"

"A hundred."

"Here." Shukri paid Milo. "Better be real good."

"You know I never let customers down. I'll be right back."

The Gypsy boy brought over their drinks. He was wearing Halid's sweater, which he had forgotten in the orchard. It fit him like a dress.

"Hey, little man," Shukri said, "I understand your friend over here gave you some money."

"He is not my friend. My friends are smart enough not to be swindled."

The men laughed, nudging each other, and toasted. The third and the fourth drinks were gone. Halid's throat was prickly.

"What did Ghurge mix his *rakija* with?" he asked. "Steel wool?"

The drinks were helping him relax and forget that his mother was probably still up waiting for him to arrive, not three miles away. He looked at Shukri's pale hand that rapped on the table and the big grin on his face. He was eyeing one of the Gypsy girls dancing in front of the band.

"Another shot! Quickly!" he ordered. It arrived at the same time as the message that Milo wanted to meet them in the back.

WHILE THE ARMY OVERLOOKED THE CLOSING OF THE factory, the local authorities insisted they build separate lavatories and not mix with the workers. Close contact between soldiers and workers often meant trouble. Instead of building lavatories, the army dragged several white construction trailers to the site and converted them into officer and NCO bathrooms. They used big oilcans as toilets and had the Gypsies dispose of the contents in the Dumanija River every Saturday. When the war started, the officers' trailer was converted into the army archive and eventually set on fire right before the retreat. The NCO trailer was left un-touched.

Milo was standing outside the metal door with a short, skinny girl on his left who couldn't have been more than fifteen. The windows behind him were lit, and Halid could see the empty file cabinets along the walls inside.

"It's getting cold again," Milo said, pulling his hands up his sleeves.

Halid and Shukri didn't respond.

Milo tried the trailer door.

"Fuck," he yelled as he shook the doorknob. "The bastard locked me out again. I owe him some money. We'll have to climb in through the window."

The window was not high, and the men crawled in easily—Milo first with Halid and Shukri behind him.

"Hey," a tiny voice shrieked. "Don't forget me."

The girl was wearing high heels and a dress too big for her that tangled around her legs as she climbed. Milo had to help her up. Halid watched as she carefully struggled to free her dress from the nail on the window's ledge. Her fingers were too long and uncoordinated, so she finally yanked the dress impatiently and let out a quiet curse, "Goddamn it," when a piece tore off.

The older prostitutes Halid met in Sarajevo were craftier, their movements more deliberate. This was a child. Halid be-grudged Shukri for convincing him to come along. He was never comfortable with prostitutes, especially the young ones.

The lavatory was big, with portable showers on one side and sinks on the other. The wall above the sinks was mirrored. Milo kicked the door open with one blow.

"I'll wait outside," he said before he left.

Shukri led the girl over to the right sink, when he noticed that the mirror was cracked.

"Shit, this will bring me bad luck. I can't do it here under a broken mirror."

"Cover it," Halid said.

"With what?"

"With something."

Shukri turned to the girl. "Lift your arms up," he ordered, and pulled her dress over her head. The girl wrapped her arms around her breasts. Shukri stuck the dress over the top of the mirror and covered the crack.

"How's this?"

Then he shoved the girl over the sink. Halid looked at the dark, knobby vertebrae that protruded through her wax-colored skin and followed her spine as it curved down and vanished inside her underwear.

"Lift up your leg," Shukri said. The girl did what she was told. Shukri pulled her panties down with his foot and mounted her leg over the sink.

Halid watched from the doorway. The girl looked funny with one leg up. Shukri picked up a *flajterka*, a spray bottle that was left in every military bathroom for Muslim soldiers to wash themselves after they used the toilet. He sprayed the girl between her legs. Startled, she tried to get away, but Shukri pushed her back down and sprayed her in the back of her head. She cried out.

"Shukri, don't," Halid said. "Either do your business or let her go."

Shukri turned around in disbelief. "What are you talking about?"

"What are you doing?"

"I'm doing what I paid for. She is a fucking Gypsy *Kaur*. They don't wash after they shit. Want me to catch something?"

"I'm just telling you to go easy."

"I can go easy on my wife. I already paid to do what I want to do."

"No, I did. Remember? Let her go."

"I thought that money was supposed to be a gift."

"Not for shit like this."

"Who are you? The savior?" Shukri's sweaty face reddened. "Butt out."

Shukri unzipped his pants and soon he was pushing in and out of the girl, rocking back and forth, lifting her heels off the ground.

Suddenly he slapped her hard across the back, and she screamed.

"Shut up." He slapped her again.

Halid dove toward Shukri and grabbed him by the arm. "Stop it!"

Shukri looked at him as if he had forgotten he was there.

"Stay back," Shukri growled.

"No. Let her go."

Shukri hit the girl again. She didn't make any noise this time, but she visibly tensed up.

"See, she's quiet. She likes it."

Halid grabbed Shukri by the hips and yanked him away from the girl.

"What are you doing?" Shukri was furious.

"Let her go."

"What's your problem?"

"That's wrong."

"Says who?" Shukri asked.

"I say."

"She is a *Ciganchina*. A darky Christian. Half human. What are you, a saint? A traitor? What's next—you're going to cross yourself and eat the dirty *domuz*? Is that what we fought for?"

"At least I stayed until the end of the war and fought."

Shukri took a swing at him. Halid had expected it and got out of the way. With his pants down, Shukri stumbled, lost his balance, and fell to the ground.

"Fuck," he yelled as he looked at his knuckles. One of them was bleeding. Halid tried to help him up. Shukri refused his arm.

"Come on, man, just let her go," Halid was pleading. "She's not worth the fight."

Without turning, Shukri said to the girl, "Get out of here."

She pulled her panties up, grabbed her dress off the mirror, and ran toward the door, leaving one of her shoes behind.

Shukri stood up. "What's the matter with you?"

"Let's just go and have another drink," Halid said.

"You go first. I'll be right there. I need to wash myself."

"What an asshole," Halid heard behind him as stepped through the door.

The Gypsy boy was sitting on the fence next to the trailer, rocking his legs. He had taken Halid's sweater off. The fence was close enough for him to have heard everything. In all the time he had visited the various whorehouses, Halid had never had to face any prostitute's family.

"She forgot her shoe inside," Halid said. He had never been more embarrassed in his life.

AS SOON AS HE SAT BACK IN HIS CHAIR, ANOTHER DRINK arrived. He threw it down. This one was smoother. It didn't burn his throat as much. The buzz of the music and the blurred Gypsy faces swirled around him.

Shukri didn't return until Halid was finished with the next round. Nothing gave away their exchange except the whiteness around Shukri's tightly held knuckles and some drying blood on his fingers. Shukri sat down without a glimpse at Halid and motioned another girl toward the table. This one was a little older. Maybe twenty. Shukri stuck his hand under her skirt. She sighed. He pulled his hand out, smelled, and said "ripe." Everybody who saw, including the girl, laughed. Then the next round, a double, landed on the table. Before Halid could reach for the glass, Shukri dipped his fingers in.

"Drink," he said.

Halid knocked the glass off the table with his Luger; it shattered on the floor.

"I know what's going on," Shukri said. "Gypsy pussy's not good enough for you? You want that blond *Kaur*, Mira, don't you?" Shukri finished a shot.

"What's it to you?"

"Everything. I need to know what side you're on."

Lale came over to the table and looked at Shukri's bleeding hand. Then he spat on the floor.

"If you were older," Shukri laughed, "I'd kick your ass."

"If I were older," Lale said, "I'd kill you."

Shukri tried to nab Lale, but the boy was too quick for a drunken man to catch. He spat again as he left the barrack, and Halid and the girl laughed.

"Go to him," Shukri ordered the girl. "Maybe he'll take some from you." The girl twirled before she rubbed up against Halid.

"So, soldier," she said, as she sat on his lap. "I heard you came back heavy with cash."

"Uh-huh," Halid answered, as he crawled his fingers underneath her shirt.

"Ask him where he got his money," Shukri said to the girl.

Halid rubbed the girl's breasts. They were hard and wet. She was nursing.

"You can ask me too." Shukri leaned the girl back and lifted her shirt. Halid could see the dilated veins on the skin around her nipples. Shukri put his thumb and an index finger around one and squeezed a drop into his *rakija* glass.

Halid tried to stand up. Then the girl reached her hand toward his chest. Halid pushed her away. Tingles rippled through his stomach. Shukri emptied his glass, threw it over his shoulder, leaned close to Halid's ear, and said, "I know where you got the money from. If you want me to keep my mouth shut, you'll have to give me some."

Then there was another double in front of Halid. He swallowed it without looking at Shukri. The girl had gone. The room slowly spun around him, and he tried to focus on the wall to make it stop. "Where in Sarajevo did you fight?" somebody asked. The hum of a violin erased his answer. Then he forgot the question, but he didn't care; he had been distracted by the flash of a youthful white thigh and a short red skirt. A different woman moved close to him and asked, how loaded are you? "Pretty loaded," he replied. No, somebody said, maybe Shukri, the missiles don't light up the sky like that, what are you talking about? It's more red than yellow. Another white limb appeared, older than the first leg, saggier and dry skinned. A drink followed. His glass touched his lips. Then the wood from the table reached his cheek. Then all was dark.

7

HE OPENED HIS EYES AND ROLLED UP IN A
ball against the morning chill, smelling of cigarettes and *rakija*. A nasty tart taste clung to his palate. The sun was well
over the eastern peak—it was probably past six o'clock. He
couldn't remember how he got back to the orchard or what
he did the last few hours of the night. As he twisted on the
ground to find a comfortable position for his shoulder, he felt
a lump the size of a brick pressing against his chest. He had a
carton of Rothmans in his pocket. He hoped that alcohol

hadn't stupefied him to the point of paying for such garbage. He tried to get up. With both his knees still on the ground and his good arm supporting the weight of his body, he remembered Shukri whispering, "I know where you got the money from."

Still on all fours, Halid tensed up. Shukri wasn't even in Sarajevo that month. Who could have told him? Someone else from his platoon? Couldn't be. All seasoned fighters kept their mouths shut, and none were great friends of Shukri's.

How he regretted that shot. One shot out of thousands had to go in the wrong direction. He had fired and missed plenty during combat. In war, death was a matter of good aim. Why couldn't he have missed this time? The girl fell to the floor gently, as if pushed in a child's game. Her coat opened to show a lovely turquoise scarf carefully tied around her graceful neck. She lay so prettily, so inviting on her back, her knees slightly parted. Her hair and the fringe on the scarf spread around her like petals on a flower.

He tried to stop the blood with his hands, but it relentlessly gushed from her forehead, erasing her features. Her neck became limp, her head heavy. Then he recognized the scarf. "The little hero," the entrenched soldiers called the pretty girl that boldly walked the besieged streets of Sarajevo and smiled at everyone. The daughter of the only highly ranked Muslim officer from Halid's town, Colonel Mashan. Completely devoted to his soldiers, the colonel moved his entire family and two of his watchdogs to Sarajevo, despite the bombing. Defiant like her father, pretty Aida tempted fate and snipers with her bright colors. Soldiers whistled at the colonel's lovely daughter, always trying to capture her attention.

Halid's luck turned bad when he broke into one of the abandoned buildings in an effort to get some sleep. She startled him from behind, coming in from the other room. He thought he was being ambushed, and he pulled his Luger and fired. Not until she was on the floor did he realize his mistake.

It was a terrible accident. He ran out of the building as fast as he could, until he reached a nearby bridge. He flung himself into the water and scrubbed himself until her blood washed off his hands and clothes.

They found her the next day. Halid hardly said a word to anyone all morning and volunteered for a raid at night. How could Shukri know what he thought no one did? Someone must have made the connection to him. It wasn't his Luger that gave him away. They were common enough. But he was one of the few on leave that afternoon, and the only one whose boots and belt were inexplicably wet for two days.

He was still propped up against his favorite plum tree when the sun passed the east peak and shone straight in his face. He did nothing to shield himself. *Rakija* always made him sluggish and dull the following day. He yanked the Rothmans out of his pocket and tossed them into the water, scaring a sparrow out of the reeds.

If Shukri knew, by now the news must have reached Mother. There would be no more hiding in the orchard, behind his family's name, his mother's skirt. He stood up and headed toward the Milosnic house.

HARDENED MUD, LEFT UNSCRUBBED AFTER SOME BIG storm, completely covered the walkway to the Milosnic house. The rubber doormat was three feet away from the step, thrown over a wilting shrub. Soot, mixed with rain, stained the maple front door, which Momir had carved and finished himself. The windows on the top floor had never been framed. Two empty black holes gaped at the street. The bench outside the front door leaned to one side. Halid remembered the many summer nights he and Momir spent sitting on the bench eating sorbet and arguing about soccer until the unbearable late-night mosquitoes chased them inside the house.

The last time he crossed the Milosnic doorstep was in '79, the first year the soccer teams were separated by religion. The Christians lost three to one. Momir, frustrated by his team's performance, kicked the glass water bottle wearing his torn-up cleats and screamed as blood poured from his toes. As Halid and Shukri carried him home, he said, "If I had as many sheep as Halid's father, I could have bought new cleats. Then I could have kicked the damn bottle and walked away." Halid and Shukri cackled, tripped, and almost dropped him.

Stana had the boys bring Momir into the kitchen and put him on the table so she could sew up his toes.

Halid stepped inside the hallway. Now, fourteen years later, it seemed too narrow to have fit Halid and Shukri carrying a grown man in their arms. He could easily reach both walls if he stood in the middle with his arms open.

He rubbed his belt, something he always did when he was nervous. The Luger jabbed into his back. He took it out to put it somewhere more comfortable, and then he realized he was holding a gun, standing inside a dead friend's house. Ashamed, he quickly pushed the Luger back into his pants.

Mira and Stana both stood at the other end of the hallway, right by the kitchen, under a row of hanging milk buckets. Neither looked surprised to see him. Mira had washed her scarf and wore a clean shirt.

"I will not stand for sneaking around," Stana said without hesitating. "She can't leave the house in the middle of the night. Not as long as she is under my roof. Do you understand me?"

"Please. I didn't come here to fight." He stretched his arms out in defense.

"Then what do you want?"

"I've come to talk about the child," he whispered.

Stana grabbed Mira by the sleeve. "So this is why you were tidying yourself all morning. For the circumcised!"

"She has nothing to do with this," he tried to explain, to protect Mira. "It was my idea! I wanted to talk about the boy."

"He is not your son," Stana yelled, walking toward Halid. "Get that stupid idea out of your head and get out of here. There is nothing to talk about."

When she reached the staircase in front of Halid, Stana halted, turned, and hurried upstairs.

"Halid," Mira warned, "she loaded Momir's old rifle this morning. Get out of here right now."

There was a shot upstairs. It was clear and it didn't hit anything. Stana had fired a warning shot through the window. Then, in a strangely calm, barely audible voice, she spoke from the top of the stairs. "This thing is working. So, get out of here before I use it."

Halid had known Stana for as long as he could remember. He knew her husband beat her more and more as her body and her face changed from childbearing. He had spent more nights at the tavern than at home. On Sundays the whole church gossiped about his Saturday night escapades. Stana bore her grief silently and never complained. Halid respected her strength. If he stayed any longer, she'd keep her word and shoot. If she kept firing the rifle, she'd get arrested. The newly formed government was weary of the armed Serbs. A woman her age would not do well in the town's jail. Halid's mother had been held overnight for questioning on the whereabouts of the family's weapons. It almost killed her. He quickly glanced at Mira and left.

STILL GRIPPING THE MAUSER, STANA HEARD THE DOOR close behind Halid. She waited, listening. Mira had stepped outside into the garden and sat by Mladen's cage with little Ivan by her feet. The boy was wearing his special occasion clothes. Stana had made his blue navy coat from one of her skirts. Mira bought the red shoes at a fair. Stana never liked the prissy shoes, but she hated the fact that Mira had dressed him in his best for Halid. What a face-staining disgrace.

The family had been dishonored by Mira before—when the whole town buzzed with the rumor of the bride's relations with the Muslim. She was seen devouring whole pickles, and the people speculated that she was heavy with Halid's seed before she married Momir.

Stana was furious and wanted to call the whole thing off, but there was no reasoning with Momir. He wanted the pretty girl. There was nothing a widowed mother could do but try to salvage their respectable name. So she lavished the precious family heirloom, the icon of Saint Jovan, on the ungrateful girl the night before the wedding, in front of all of their relatives. A gesture designed to be interpreted as an act of goodwill, confirmation that her son's choice coincided with hers. She took the icon back a week later.

Ivan ran toward Mladen's cage and swung around holding on to the bars. Mladen laughed and pretended he was trying to catch him. Then he ran back into his mother's arms. Look at that. Holding a boy like that all the time, always touching him. We are lucky if the young man inside isn't already spoiled for good. The boy needs to play rough, get in trouble. Even when Mira was away, and Stana forced him outside, he just stood by the front door, watching the other kids. Nothing like his father. Momir used to dart outside before he swallowed the last bite of his breakfast and spent the day rolling and wrestling with the other boys until hunger showed him the way back to her kitchen. Once he didn't even notice a bee sting on his arm.

What a son to be proud of. Tall, handsome, a fierce fighter, a crafty hunter. Everybody liked him. Of all the village children he was destined to amount to the most. What a waste for his son to be so cowardly and timid, shying away from his grandmother. Mira put him up to it, she was sure, but still—rejecting his own? What if the gossip was true, if the baby really wasn't Momir's? Ivan was born during the corn harvest, only seven months after the wedding, but Stana always took the early birth to be a sign of Momir's mischief.

She stared down at her feet, at her husband's boots for which she had no shoelaces. Whenever the rough hide scraped her skin she'd remember her loveless marriage. She loathed the boots as much as her dead husband, but she had no money for a new pair. All of her shoes had fallen apart.

The windowpane in her bedroom had cracked. She leaned the Mauser against it. The house was in ill repair. Everything needed fixing, but there was money for nothing. One day the house would cave in on itself and they'd all be turned out to starve like stray dogs. This business with Halid was a bad omen. She regretted not giving a coin to a begging Gypsy.

THE PRAYING CHAMBER HAD BECOME THE LEAST
frequented room in the house since the arrival of the cable
notifying the family of Momir's death. Stana didn't need Pap
to come over and read it. She knew what had happened. The
government never sent cables for the wounded. The postman
didn't act like he was waiting for his customary tip. Before he
even had the time to cross over her doorstep on his way out,
she was already blowing out the candle in front of Saint
Jovan. What she had asked for, prayed for, hadn't been
granted. As the smoke coiled above the candle, she vowed
never to worship again and spat as she shut the door forever.

And now Halid had returned and asked for the boy. She
knew that her son's Mauser and the five bullets she had saved
couldn't keep him away for long. They were all on his side
now: Mira, Rade, the police, even Pap.

Pap, with all his love of justice, still cared to save himself
first.

She used the rifle butt to push open the chamber door.
The room had remained unchanged from the days when they
were serfs huddled together on the floor praying to their
Christian God. Dust covered her icons. The gold-plated face
of Saint Jovan didn't shimmer like it used to. And Stana no
longer saved her last pennies to pay for the candles to keep
the whole room lit.

The icon had belonged to her grandmother. Her grandmother had been the pasha's concubine, *milosnica*. She was stolen for the harem at the age of thirteen. When the pasha returned her, she spent the rest of her life as a devout Christian.

She moved over to the icon of Saint George, the patron saint of the local Christian Gypsies, whom she never asked for help. Sensitive about her dark hair and her brown skin, Stana refused to be mistaken for a *Cigan*. But Saint George was the one who had slain the dragon and to whom those in danger turned.

Inside a small pouch underneath her housedress she had been hiding a candle for over a year. When she lit it, it flickered slowly. "Why didn't my boy come home and this one did?" she asked. "He was a good man. Inside, all kindness and warmth." The tears bubbled and she choked back a gasp. She didn't have the strength needed for cursing Mira and Halid, which is what she had intended. Cursing took a lot out of a person. A lot was beaten out of her the day the cable arrived. She blew out the candle. The saint's face looked back at her through the smoke. A cheap icon, she thought. No use in sitting around and crying. There were better things to do. If the baby is not Momir's, then the hell with it. Let Halid pay. She had Mladen to worry about.

As she put the candle inside her pouch she felt a boiled egg she snatched from somebody's table last Easter. The egg was beautiful, painted red and yellow, its shell still untouched. For months she carried it around, waiting for the right moment to give it to her grandson. But she had grown quite cold toward the boy, and the egg was still in her pouch completely forgotten. Now, she was afraid to eat it herself. It was probably bad.

She started to lay her forehead to the ground in front of the saint to kiss the floor as she always used to. Then she changed her mind, picked up the rifle, and left the room.

CROSSING THE STREAM WAS THE EASIEST WAY TO GET TO Pap. Naked from the waist down, holding his pants and boots above his head, Halid emerged from the water. The house was half a mile up the road. Its outside hadn't changed at all. Carefully pruned but oddly shaped cherry bushes and vines surrounded the cobblestone path, which was free of dirt. Pap was one of the few people in the village who knew how to properly lay cobblestone, and the only one who could afford it. Halid knocked on the door several times. Finally, Lale opened the door.

"What do you want?" he asked.

"Is Pap home?"

"He's sleeping."

"I'll come back later," Halid said. "Sorry about last night. Was she your sister?"

The boy's face changed. For a second Halid thought he might cry. Then his eyes narrowed with hatred. Halid withdrew, just in time to keep a huge stone from smashing his head.

"Motherfucker," Lale said, and ran away.

"What's going on?" Pap appeared.

"Nothing," Halid said. "The boy is acting up. He'll be fine. I have to talk to you."

"Come on in."

The smell of wall fungus, of the softening concrete and the piles of moldy garments, lingered heavily in the air. Pap had saved all of his children's and his wife's clothes in his closets. Back in the seventies, when things were looking up, he let Halid talk him into painting his kitchen. Halfway into the project, pale and shaken, as if he had received some terrible news, Pap resolutely told Halid that the project was finished and that there was no reason to further alter the house. Respectful of the old man's wishes, Halid never asked why.

"What can I help you with?" Pap asked. "Can I offer you some coffee?"

"No, thanks. I need you to talk to Stana for me. I tried and made a mess out of it. Now I'm afraid she'll do something silly."

"You can't blame her. She has lost too much," Pap said. "What do you want me to tell her?"

"I want you to talk to her about Mira and her son."

Pap took a sugar cube from a bowl and dipped it into his *fildzan*. The cube sucked up the liquid in the cup and turned brown. Halid thought of Mother. She always drank coffee the same way.

"Is the boy yours?" Pap asked.

"I'm not sure."

"That's a lot not to be sure about."

"Does it matter?"

"It may matter a great deal to Stana."

"There is a chance he might be."

"There were lots of rumors before you left, and he did come too soon. But the stress of war could have pushed him out early. He could still be Momir's. You don't have enough proof."

"I'm not sure," Halid said.

"Did you think to ask Mira?"

"Couldn't get myself to do it."

"You're going to have to."

"Later."

"So where do I come in?"

"I want you to persuade Stana to let me take Mira and the boy."

"You want to take the boy you're not sure is yours?"

"It makes no difference to me."

"And do what?" Pap asked.

"Leave this place."

"Where'll you go?"

"Maybe to America."

"To America? Are you sure?"

"A lot of our people went there after the war."

"A lot of mine too. But it didn't make them happy."

"How do you know that? You've never been to America."

"My brother lived there for forty years before he died." Pap paused. "All his children think about is money."

Halid had no idea that Pap's brother had passed away. They hadn't seen each other since he left for the United States some forty years before. It had to have been a huge blow.

"We are no different. We think about money too," Halid said.

"Not all of us."

"Not you," Halid said.

"You neither. You were always better than that."

"I'm not sure you're right."

"I am."

Then Lale burst through the door with so much force that both Pap and Halid stood up.

"Quick! Quick! A wolf pack broke through Shukri's fences and killed five sheep and three lambs! Made a huge, big mess! The men are forming a posse. My father is coming too. Shukri asked for Halid."

"Calm down, boy," Pap said. "There are wolves?"

"Yes, they took five sheep and three lambs. Eight total."

Pap looked at Halid. "It's probably one of those Shukri myths," he said.

"I'm going anyway." Halid knew he had to. Shukri must have a reason to summon him. He had no other choice.

"Why don't you go, and I'll talk to Stana," Pap said.

Suddenly Pap looked tired and old to Halid. His leg wasn't holding up too well. It seemed unfair to send him running around the village.

"Don't do too much," he said.

"I'll be fine. And I'll send you word if there's any progress. But I need you to do something for me too."

"What?" Halid asked.

"Go and see your mother when you're done playing with Shukri."

8

PASSING TROOPS DESTROYED THE HUNTING
camp. They tore out the table and the two benches built
around the cement grill and knocked over the rain cover. It
was a sad ending for a sacred place. For more than three centuries, hunters had gathered around the fire at night to clean
their weapons and make plans for the next day. The trackers
exchanged information. The designated cooks baked the
bread and grilled the meat for dinner. *Rakija* circled the
table, followed first by tales of hunting and eventually by war

stories. There were plenty of both to go around. Each hunter, no matter what age, had at least a bear and a war under his belt. At dawn, as the fire died, those sober enough to shoot gathered their weapons, stomped out the remaining embers, and kicked their comatose friends out of their stupor. Hanging their rifles over their shoulders, the men stuffed the warm bread inside their bags and journeyed toward the areas where the trackers reported the latest traces of game.

The hunting had been dwindling since before the war. First, the Communists cut down the forests, making the animal habitat smaller. Then the mayor of a nearby city personally declared war on wolves, branding them "public enemy number one." Huge packs used to slaughter entire flocks of sheep, tearing the throats of the guard dogs dumb enough to stick around for a fight. The villagers armed themselves with imported traps, spiked collars for the dogs' necks, and .22 Hornets with double-powered telescopic sights. As a result, the wolves retreated farther up the mountain, coming down only during the harshest winters. So few in number, they would take only a sheep or two a season at most. Occasionally Halid and Momir tried their luck at hunting, but all the predators worth killing had disappeared. Only ducks, pheasants, and rabbits survived.

By the time Halid arrived at what was left of the camp with Lale on his tail, it was well past noon. Shukri was standing in the middle of a small clearing. Ghurge was sleeping on the ground next to another man Halid didn't recognize.

"Hah," Shukri laughed. "Naked to hunt! Where is your rifle, soldier?"

"Why bother?" Halid kicked through the pile of leaves. "There is nothing around here that's legal this time of year. And what about this pack breaking through your fences?"

"Didn't you hear all that howling last night? Or maybe you were too drunk?"

Shukri was out for blood. Only Halid wasn't sure how much and how fast.

"They're close, and they're hungry. Besides, we don't need permits. The law is here with us. Meet Simo." Shukri pointed at the man next to Ghurge who was wearing a short-sleeved, dark blue police shirt, capri pants, and a gun strap on his shoulder. He must have been one of the new policemen who were transferred here after the war. He had no rifle either.

Shukri took the bottle out of his bag and offered it to Halid. "As for the story, I knew it'd get you up here."

"Did you sleep?" Halid asked.

"No, I'll go home after my wife's gone to the fields. She does nothing but nag anyway, and I don't want to hear it. Today I want to hunt."

"With what? We have no dogs. We don't even have a rifle."

"We'll tie a lamb somewhere," Shukri said, and Halid lost his patience.

"For a wolf, in the middle of the day? And leave our smells all over the place. Maybe you could sniff them out yourself, or maybe the policeman can do it." He took another huge gulp of *rakija*.

"I heard of a guy who took a wolf down with a nine millimeter," Shukri said.

"It was actually my mother," Halid said.

He turned to Simo and Ghurge. "Mr. John Wayne over here thinks he is in the movies," he said. "He means to catch a wolf with just a lamb in the middle of the day."

Ghurge slapped his hand against his thigh. His stocky body trembled with laughter. "Mr. John Wayne! Mr. John Wayne!"

Simo shook his head and said, "I can't believe I let you talk me into this."

Shukri wasn't ready to give up. "I guess the wolf is smart enough not to attack an innocent lamb in the middle of the day? Smarter than some people." He looked angrily at Halid.

Ghurge stopped laughing. Simo didn't react. At least now Halid knew how far Shukri had spread the word about the girl in one morning. Ghurge knew: Simo did not. Halid pulled his Luger out and said, "All right, let's do it."

Since the lamb strategy crumbled, the men agreed to try an alternative. They would separate into two groups: Halid and Simo in one, Shukri and Ghurge in the other. Shukri and Ghurge would raise as much noise as possible and lift pheasants and ducks from the bushes toward Halid and Simo, who would be ready to shoot. Halid knew there would be no ducks around at this time of year and that the pheasants were scarce. So did Shukri, he was sure. Nevertheless, he decided to go along with Shukri's farce for as long as it lasted. At least he had a bottle.

THE OCTOBER DAMP HAD HEAVIED THE LEAVES. THE woods were quiet. Shukri and Ghurge occasionally badly imitated the call of a duck. Halid looked up at the muddy sky and saw a few black dots flying above him. Too small to be anything worthwhile. Probably crows. A bird cried out. Halid shivered. The air hadn't warmed up yet, and it probably wouldn't for a while. He lit a cigarette and exhaled. His sweater was itchy and his legs had not loosened up despite all the walking.

The forest was thickening with pines. Nobody cut timber this far away from town. It was impossible to drag it back. He and Simo hadn't exchanged a word since they left the others. Simo was leading and Halid followed the back of his police cap, avoiding low branches. It was nearing two o'clock.

Ten minutes later, Simo suggested they stop combing the bushes and look for animal tracks on the ground.

"Combing?" Halid asked. "Did any wolves escape from the police station?"

"You're lucky you're Shukri's friend."

"Some luck."

He lit another cigarette. What a waste of a day. They would find nothing. Even if there were tracks, neither Halid nor Simo was experienced enough to interpret them.

The only one who could really track was Momir. A skilled

hunter, Momir would leave rabbit traps all over the woods while he went fox hunting with his dogs high up on the mountain. By the morning there would be half a dozen rabbits to take home. The extras were always given away. Once, Momir shot a buck, and Halid and Shukri helped carry it back. To thank them, Momir split it three ways.

Shukri hollered again—this time, with less determination. Maybe he too was getting tired of the charade. Having hungover Ghurge as a companion couldn't be too comforting.

Simo bent over a pile of twigs to check something, lost his balance, and landed clumsily on a large dry branch. It cracked in two, and one of the pieces cut a gash in his shin.

"Shit!" he yelped.

Halid couldn't help laughing. Shukri's little policeman in his cute pants assaulted and defeated by a dry branch. Perfect. Where is Shukri now? Oh, to see his boy on his ass. Simo's leg was bleeding a little, but the wound was superficial.

"You'll live," Halid said.

"Give me the bottle."

"Here." Halid thought Simo was going to have a sip. Instead he poured *rakija* over his leg.

"Easy with that." Halid jerked the bottle out of his hands.

"I don't want an infection."

"From a little scratch? You're not wasting booze on that."

Shukri's duck calls echoed through the woods. This time closer.

"He screams like a horny woman," Simo said. "That's not going to scare a sparrow."

"Shukri will raise some birds," Halid responded in Shukri's defense.

"Shush, I hear something hissing." Simo pointed his chubby white finger in the direction of a fallen log.

The log leaned against a tall oak. Shrubs grew around it, giving it the appearance of a huge bulging root from a neighboring tree. The summer humidity had dried and darkened the bark completely and covered it with black moss. Nothing with flesh worth eating could be living there.

"If you can hear it," Halid said, "it's probably sick. And it can't be anything good enough to shoot."

"We'll find out," Simo said. He climbed up on the log and kicked around the hole. Then he lay on top of the trunk and pecked through the hole in the middle.

"Something was hissing, I'm sure. Maybe a *poskok.*"

"Snakes don't hiss so loudly. It's probably a burrowing owl. Leave it."

Simo fired three shots inside the trunk. The hissing stopped. He checked the hole again. Then he stuck his hand through and dragged the wounded owl out. It wasn't dead yet. The bird tried to grab a piece of bark with its beak. Halid looked away. Even at its best, the burrowing owl merely skirted the territory of its majestic cousin, the *chuk,* the taloned master hunter that dominated this area at night and could be heard for miles. Long-legged and awkward, the burrowing owl had terrible vision and lived in the trunks of fallen trees, feeding on carrion during the day. If hunting wolves was the summit of the hunter's achievements, and shooting ducks and pheasants more of a casual hobby like fishing, then killing a clumsy bird with a police revolver was a complete ignominy.

The still eye of the dying bird was looking at Halid. He took his Luger out and unlocked the safety gauge.

"Did you guys get something?" Ghurge and Shukri ran up, the latter with a nine-millimeter semiautomatic in his hand. Lale was maybe fifty feet behind.

"This idiot shot an owl," Halid yelled at Shukri.

"Who's an idiot?" Simo pointed his gun at Halid. "I heard the hissing. So did you. It could have been a snake."

"I told you that a fucking snake doesn't make a sound like that." Halid thought about how well his fist would fit Simo's flabby chin.

"Take it easy, everybody!" Shukri yelled, his eyes on Halid's gun.

"What a fucking idiot," he said to Shukri, clutching the butt with both hands and raising the gun halfway up. "Tell me, Shukri, since when did we become friends with the police and the *Cigani*?"

"It's just a bird," Shukri said. "Just a bird."

"Go fuck yourself."

By the time Halid realized Ghurge was not in his field of vision, he was on the ground and his Luger had been kicked out of his hands. Shukri picked it off the ground and emptied the charger. Then he pointed his gun at the bird. "Is this what's wrong?" He leaned close to Halid's ear. "Do you want me to put it out of its misery?"

"Shoot, goddamn you," Halid said.

Shukri fired all ten bullets. The blasts disintegrated the bird.

"All right, that's taken care of. Let's go back now, I'm hungry," Shukri said.

Tears dimmed Halid's vision. Before him was a stranger. He picked the Luger, the charger, and the bullets off the ground and put them back inside his pocket. He gulped the leftover liquor. His throat and eyes were burning. He flung the bottle as far as he could.

"Now what?" Shukri asked.

Halid had no energy for Shukri. Without looking at him, he started back toward the village.

"Where do you think you're going?" Shukri hollered behind. Halid kept on walking.

HE FOLLOWED THE TRAIL THROUGH THE WOODS FOR A while, and then crossed the creek back to the pastures. Behind a fence, a few scattered sheep and cows grazed. On the other side, a young horse chained to a stake by its foreleg rummaged through the wet leaves and mud. The horse was probably confiscated from its rightful owner; only someone green about horses would tie an eighteen-hundred-pound animal by its most frail part.

The horse was by no means spectacular. His back was too long and sloping, his hind hollow and covered in dry manure, the legs over at the knee. His mane had never been pulled. Nothing like the *über* specimens Halid saw during his military training. Yet there was something comforting in the way he didn't notice Halid or swish his tail nervously like a warhorse. Oblivious to the world, he simply flicked his ears occasionally to chase away the flies.

One of the cows came to the fence and scratched its horns against it—a daily ritual signaling the time to return to the barn for the evening feeding and milking. The horse lifted his snout and snorted. Then he dropped his head down and continued to graze. He would probably stop feeding at nightfall and wait to be taken to the barn for some grain.

Father's grave was right next to the pastures. Halid looked at the graveyard and stumbled. The *rakija* had muffled his head. He had drunk too much, without eating. "Always save the bad things for when you've had enough *rakija*. Just be careful if your stomach is empty," he remembered Father's motto.

According to his wishes, Father was buried in the largest Muslim graveyard with the rest of his family. The grass on his grave was fresh, the soil still elevated. There was no tombstone, just a cement Turkish turban on top of a rectangular stone—the latest fashion. Father would have been outraged if he could see the twirly thing. A zealous Communist, the old man hated religion and probably wished to be laid out under a red star.

The sight of a grave was old news. Halid had helped dig too many, some in bad weather, in a blizzard, in the pouring rain. This evening was turning out to be beautiful. The cold breeze blew his hair and freshened his nostrils. He couldn't muster up pity for the old man.

Father had died of a heart attack while Halid was fighting. The first in the family. Only women died of natural causes, usually of some belly ailment. All male relatives died young in previous wars. Halid knew them only through Father's embellished family war stories. They either choked on or slipped in their own blood as they drew their last heroic breaths, taking at least a dozen enemies with them. For Father, that was the picture of a perfect death.

It was different for Halid. The masses of soldiers that poured down from the villages throughout Bosnia humming their ancestral war songs with lyrics slightly altered to fit the times, but with the same lust for blood, seemed senseless and stupid. War was their only way, they claimed, the way of their fathers and of their fathers' fathers. They had little regard for the living. The images of their heroic ancestors' throats slit by the enemy's knives, enhanced by the incessant *rakija* drinking, drove them to the madness of bravery. It was true that their deaths seemed preordained, but it still made no sense.

Halid wondered if the old man's dying had been drawn

out, if he knew it was coming. A heart attack usually took a man's life in a matter of minutes. He couldn't remember their last conversation, only the last bar fight, just two weeks before the war started. A new bartender at the local bus station bar publicly insulted the old man, called him a drunken fool. He had no idea that his son and a friend sat at the other end of the counter. When Momir and Halid's bar stools crashed against his newly stacked bottles, he gaped in amazement. It cost Mother a small fortune—three turkeys and a calf—to repay the damage. Bleeding from their laughing mouths—the bartender had good fists and knew how to use them—Momir and Halid tossed the old man in the back of the carriage and drove him home, singing.

Father was snoring when Momir mentioned his upcoming nuptials.

"Are you sure you're okay with it?" he asked.

"Yes. Mira and I've been finished for a while now. And it was never that big of a thing."

"It all happened so fast," Momir said. "They say the war is about to start. I think her old man is worried about all of us dying, so he wants to see her settled."

"Is that why you're getting married?"

"No. I like her a lot. She's beautiful."

"That she is."

That morning Halid had received word that Mira wanted to see him.

"You're going to be my best man, right?" Momir asked.

"I can't."

"Why?"

"Things have been so bad around here. A Muslim standing up for a Serb may cause more trouble than we can handle."

Momir halted the horse. Father muttered something.

"But you're coming to my wedding?"

"Better I don't."

"Really?"

"There'll be a lot of celebratory shots. I don't want one of your cousins to turn me into a colander by mistake."

"That would make you a holy man." Momir elbowed him, laughing.

Too honorable to be suspicious, Momir clucked at the horse and seemed satisfied with Halid's answer. Halid went hunting the next day and stayed away for a week.

"HEY, SOLDIER!" LALE HAD SNUCK UP BEHIND HALID. "I've been looking for you everywhere." The boy had no jacket on and the wind blew the collar on his shirt. He was shifting from one foot to the other to keep warm.

"Why don't you wear my sweater?"

"I threw it away. Pap sent me to tell you that Stana is ready to talk."

"He talked her into it already?"

"What?" The boy didn't understand.

"Never mind. Go back and tell them that I'll be over soon."

"Pap said to stay with you. He heard you had a fight with Shukri. He said you might do something stupid."

Halid smiled. "Don't you know that soldiers always do stupid things?"

"Yeah, like what?"

"Like the thing with your sister. That was stupid and I want to apologize."

Lale backed off angrily. "Why don't you just shut up and go see Pap," he said.

As Lale ran, the horse snorted and arched his neck. The chain around his leg pulled taut. He bucked but the stake didn't give. The horse reared. The stake still didn't budge. If the poor thing hurt his leg, he would have to be put down. And now that weapons were strictly forbidden for those who were not in the forces, the owner couldn't even shoot him and get it over with quickly.

The owner would have to use the good old butcher hammer. If skilled enough at killing, he'd render the horse unconscious with the first blow. Halid imagined a broad man's forearm with a callused elbow striking the blow, the animal falling to his front knees tearing his halter to shreds, his bleeding muzzle hitting the wooden board beneath it.

What did he care about a thing like a horse? It was a working animal, destined to haul and plow, and occasionally to breed more of its kind to do exactly the same. The dead girl was haunting him. If only he had just wounded her. If only he had a mind to aim for the leg, he'd still be in Sarajevo, maybe even working, and the mad feeling in his stomach, the relentless flutter that kept him awake at night if he had nothing to drink, would subside.

He had only one Marlboro left, and he regretted getting rid of that carton of Rothmans earlier. The smoke would chase these unsettling thoughts away, but he'd have to save the last one for later.

9

THE DIRT CATTLE PATH THAT CONNECTED
the Milosnic house with the pastures snaked through the former Muslim neighbor's apple grove. Instead of supporting the winners of World War II, the Communists, the neighbors sided with Independent Croatia's Fascist state—a crime Father and the rest of the Communist partisans could not forgive. The male members escaped to Australia after the war, leaving behind the matriarch, an infant son, and two unmarried daughters. As an example of what happens to the traitors

of the new regime, the women and children were court-martialed and executed, their property confiscated in the name of the people, and their house torched. Inebriated with the seductive mantra of the Revolution that promised power over the oppressors, the villagers brought farming equipment to help the Communist partisans knock over the chimney. With scythes, shovels, spades, pickaxes, plows, and hoes, the chimney was leveled, and only a three-foot-tall circle of bricks still stubbornly stood above ground. The exhausted men claimed victory over the enemy and placed the youngest member of the village, the newborn from the Red Muslim Mashan family, above the still-smoking hearth, despite the protest of the baby's terrified mother.

Father never admitted to regretting his participation in the neighbor's unfortunate fate, although he had grown up with the boys and was rumored to have been sweet on one of the girls who was hanged. "Friendship leads to nepotism." He stuck to the Party line when Halid first and last inquired about the incident. "It was my duty not to feel a thing."

Above Halid's head, the yellowing branches were entangled over the path. In the summer when the trees were in full bloom, sunshine barely penetrated the leaves in needle-thin rays, and the road seemed like a magical emerald tunnel, with the lower branches reaching down to the ground.

The path was imbedded with pieces of red clay, a reminder of Turkish times when the Ottomans paved the roads with shattered brick. Halid had dug them out and used them as chalk for drawing funny figures on the outside concrete wall of their barn. Mira loved them.

An apple had fallen on the ground. Its skin was dried up and hard. An old apple was not what he needed on an empty stomach after last night's drinking. Still, he took a bite. It quickly fell apart in his mouth. He swallowed a little and spit out the rest. "Disgusting." He almost flung it away. Then he remembered that Mother was less than fifty feet away. Nobody could hear noise outside as well as Mother. She could be in the kitchen on the other side of the house and hear Father's approach. "I can feel his drunken breath vibrating in the air. Like a bat," she swore. He crammed the apple into his pocket, next to his Luger, and continued on quietly.

Beyond the next few oaks he could see the outside wall of their barn. The vines had thrown a thick coat over it since he had left. That meant dense, juicy leaves to absorb the summer heat and cool off the barn. The few summers before the war had been hot and humid, and the cattle had to be brought into the kitchen. With its four windows and a huge door, it was the draftiest room in the house. The only time the cows could be grazed was early in the morning, or at dusk after the mosque had lit its lights to mark the ending of the daily fast during the month of Ramadan.

Vines that thick must have pretty deep roots. It would take a whole day of digging to pull them out. A heavy job, even for a man, and certainly too much for Mother.

Pap was standing outside Stana's house. His face was

ashen. He hadn't a long road ahead and had more than earned his peace.

"How's your leg holding up?" Halid asked.

"It's good that you came quickly," Pap said. "How was the hunting?"

"Terrible."

"Did you get anything?"

"We had no rifles. Just guns."

"Guns?" Pap laughed.

"And Shukri brought a policeman along."

"Policeman?" Pap stopped laughing. "I wonder what's on his mind."

"I don't know yet."

"Nothing good, I'm sure. Be careful."

Halid glanced at Mother's windows. The white curtain on her window was still. Nothing in the darkness behind it gave any indication of a concealed shadow, and yet Halid was sure that she was there, watching. Pap looked at the window too: he knew that she was there as well. If they lingered, they ran a risk of Mother construing it as an invitation. Although she firmly believed that men should handle their affairs alone without any female prying, no doubt she'd break her rules after missing Halid for so long. Pap silently motioned Halid inside.

The afternoon sun shone through the front door and onto the walls. The slow whistle of the dying afternoon wind and the receding hum of the tiring crickets pulsated through the hallway. Halid and Pap entered the living room on the other side of the house. A wooden bench covered with red blankets wrapped around the wall. The two windows overlooking the garden had built-in window seats. One of the pillows, a faded green and yellow veteran from more prosperous days, was still imprinted from the seat's last occupant. A couple of elaborately etched *dzezvas* and *fildzans*—used only on special occasions for serving coffee to distinguished guests— adorned a low copper table. Made by hand, the set would be worth a fortune in foreign markets. Here, it was worth nothing. A Turkish rug covered the center of the floor. The curving crimson and deep brown pattern was handwoven in luscious silk—nothing like the cheap nylon Macedonian knockoffs worth fifteen, maybe twenty deutsche marks on the black market. This rug was worth a lot here or abroad. If Stana could afford to hold on to it, maybe she was not as desperate as he thought.

Stana determinedly marched into the living room with combed hair and a tightly buttoned, ruffled, dark blue dress—probably the best she had. Trickles of sweat dripped under Halid's armpits and behind his knees.

Not in any hurry, Stana strolled about the room, fluffed the pillow on the window seat, straightened the fringes on the rug with her toes, sat down on the sofa, and folded her legs underneath her with patience and assurance. When she finally faced her visitors, without offering them seats, there was no trace of panic on her face: she was ready.

"My son paid a great deal for that rug," she said.

"Everybody knew that *rahmetly* Momir was capable," Pap said reverently.

Stana winced at Pap's slipping in the Muslim *rahmetly* rather than the Christian *may he rest in peace*. She was coerced into this meeting. She had suspected that Pap would take Halid's side, and now it was confirmed. Swapping the *rahmet* for *rest* was an open insult. Pap was no longer backing her. She was fighting on two fronts.

"I didn't promise anything," she said, "except to talk."

"That's fine," Halid agreed. The last thing on his mind was provoking her anger. "Let's talk."

"So," she asked, "is the boy really yours?"

No one could accuse Stana of being indirect. Halid had expected her to strategize at least a little, size up the enemy, especially after she figured that normally neutral Pap had crossed over to Halid's side.

"I don't know," he said.

"Then why are you here?"

Outside the window a bush bobbed in the mild wind.

"Answer me, goddamn you!" She angrily unraveled her legs, stretching the buttonholes.

"Stana, slow down!" Pap jumped in. "Sit down, please! Is this how you receive people?"

"Receive people?" Stana glared at Pap. "Are you out of your mind? You think he's welcome in this house?"

"I thought at least I was."

"And I thought that you'd never side with the killers. And he's a killer." Her voice shook. "Just like those killers who killed your own. Or have you forgotten them?"

She was not to be trifled with today.

"Stana!" Pap raised his voice, something he almost never did. "Soldiers die in war. That's what happens."

"He fought for the other side. That's enough for me."

She was right. Disabling the mines in secret made no difference. And, as the rules of courage and shame dictated here, if he confessed, Stana and Pap would see him only as a traitor or a weakling who lacked the gall to fight. Even Momir would be outraged.

Stana readjusted her sleeves and reached for a bottle from behind her pillow.

"Here, so you don't go around saying Stana doesn't know how to welcome people in her house. Drink." She aimed the neck at Pap. "Homemade wine. Bitter like venom. Too much rain soured the grapes."

"No, thank you," Pap declined.

"How about you, lover boy?" she asked Halid.

Halid accepted. He could no longer tolerate the dance of negotiation with a dry mouth. He swallowed a few gulps. Pap watched silently. A wide, triumphant grin separated Stana's lips. No well-mannered guest would ever consider drinking straight from the bottle before he was offered a glass. Nerves took over, and Halid rushed to grab the drink before obeying the custom. A man too fond of *rakija* was a man who had lost his way.

"So," she asked again, regaining her confidence. "You think the kid's yours? Why?"

The wine was awful, and it didn't mix well with the *rakija* burning in his stomach. The wind had changed direction in the garden and the branches thumped against the window-pane. It was a dull sound. Like a stifled scream. His toes were cramping.

"Did you hear me?" she repeated.

"Why don't we ask Mira?" Pap interjected.

"Mira?" Stana hissed. "I don't even want to see her face."

"This can't be solved without her," Pap insisted.

"You can go and get her, but I'm telling you, it'll be my decision."

"I'll be right back," Pap said.

Stana faced the window with her back to Halid and sighed sadly. He pricked up his ears to hear if she was crying. The only sound he could make out was the droning ticking against the window, rhythmic as a clock. If she was, she was keeping it private. Proud as always. He remembered how the veil her husband forced her to wear stuck to her face during his fu-neral, as if the wind and the rain were blowing directly at her, although it was a very sunny day. Years later, as he watched the endless rivers of people—their faces enveloped in black to hide their unimaginable grief from the curious spectators— follow perpetual funeral processions in Sarajevo, he realized that Stana had been crying.

"You miserable Muslim bastard," she whispered, turning

toward him. "You won't always be able to hide behind someone. One day payback will come."

"I know."

"Maybe even sooner than you think," she said, and turned
away again. Her wrinkled face strained to keep calm, as if this
was just a regular visit, as if Halid had come over, as he had
many years ago, to fetch Momir to play, and she had simply
made a casual comment on the weather and advised them to
be sure to come home if it started to rain. "Boys, boys, be
careful not to catch your death wearing wet clothes," she
warned, long after the two dashed toward the soccer fields,
back then, when she cared for them both.

He closed his eyes and waited for the burning in his throat
to pass. He wanted to touch her wiry white hair and whisper
gently that everything could still turn out for the best. After
all, she was Momir's mother. She had suffered and lost the
most.

"I am so sorry," he said, not sure she could hear him. "So,
so sorry."

MIRA SHADOWED PAP. THE COLOR OF HER SKIN WAS
softened by the afternoon light. She seemed even thinner in
the roomy gray shirt she was wearing, but her new frailty no
longer bothered Halid. The hollowness around her cheek-
bones added length to her face. She looked very different
from the way he remembered her, wiser, as if she had traveled
or read important books. But still beautiful.

"Is the boy Halid's?" Stana asked as soon as Mira walked through the door.

Mira sought Pap's help, but Pap was quiet. He too wanted to know the truth.

"Well?" Stana said.

"Yes, he is," Mira said.

"Whore!" Stana screamed.

"Stana!" Pap tried to stop her.

"Stana, what? Nothing! You'd feel the same." She turned to Mira. "I want you and the little Muslim bastard out of my house. Now! And you"—she pointed at Halid—"remember, if she did this to my son, she'll do it to you too." She pounded her foot against the floor. "But not until I get a new tractor."

"You don't need a new one. A used one will do," Pap said.

"Maybe some other kid will do, too. This one he'll get for the price of a new tractor. He can have the whore for free."

"She can have a new tractor," Halid said.

"It will cost close to two thousand," Pap said.

"I don't care how much it costs. It had better be here soon," Stana said.

As she stood up she popped the last two buttons on her dress. Her white knees and thighs were exposed. Any other decent woman from around here would be mortified. Stana held her head up proudly: nobody in the room was worth her shame.

"And don't try anything stupid, like to bamboozle me or anything," she said to Halid. "If you do, I promise I'll go to every relative of yours, every person you ever met around here, and make sure that all the water in the world doesn't wash the stain off you and your whore's face."

With even greater force than when she entered, Stana left the room.

Pap walked up to Mira, who was still standing with her head down.

"Are you okay?"

She nodded.

"The two of you talk things over. You come and see me later," he said to Halid.

Mira and Halid stood without moving. The wind had altered its direction again, clearing a view of the top of Mladen's cage. It was an odd place for a cage, but it was the only area in the yard big enough. Stana had insisted it be built low to the ground, with short bars, so her guests would not be inconvenienced with the view while they were enjoying their coffee. Indeed, seen from this angle it could easily have been taken for a henhouse, with perched turkeys or chickens inside.

Halid wanted to ask Mira if she was sure he was Ivan's father, but the way her shoulders narrowed and almost swallowed her head prevented him. She had hashed out enough troubles for one day.

"Listen," he said, "get some rest, and I'll come back in the morning."

"Why are you doing this?" Mira asked and touched his arm.

"Why?" he repeated. "Why? Because I care."

His whole body felt like a fresh scar, with nothing left to give. He needed to be away. Out of here. He turned toward the door.

"Please wait," she called.

Five years ago he would have killed for those sweet words.

ONCE IN FRONT OF THE HOUSE, HE LIT HIS LAST CIGARETTE. He inhaled deeply and watched as the cigarette tip brightened and darkened, and he listened to the slow hiss of the tobacco sizzling. The sound of a wet hoof hitting the cobblestones made him look up. A young unfamiliar herdsman was bringing the cows back from the watering hole. It would be dark soon.

Without a doctor they couldn't know for sure if the boy was his. It didn't matter. The truth was, he'd probably love Momir's child more than he would his own. He loved Momir far more than he loved himself. Sons grow up to be just like their fathers. And like his father before him, his own son would amount to nothing.

He took the leftover money out of his pocket. The sun had dropped behind the Dinara's peak. He had less than nine hundred left, and it wouldn't change by morning, unless he could make a miracle. Perhaps Pap could help. Or better yet—suddenly gambling seemed like a good idea. Maybe his luck would change. And he needed a beer to soothe his nausea.

The door to his house cracked open. Mother was ready to emerge. He threw down his cigarette and walked around toward the Milosnic barn before Mother had a chance to call his name.

IT HAD BEEN SUCH A LONG WHILE SINCE HE HAD SMELLED the cattle. He could understand why city people grimaced as the first whiff of manure offended their nostrils. The air was bitter from the stench of the manure and cow piss.

"Halid."

Mira had followed him.

"Yes?" he answered, reluctant to turn.

"You weren't leaving, were you?"

"What do you mean, leaving?" he asked. "I'm not going anywhere."

The zipper on her shirt was pulled farther down and he could see her bare bony chest and her heart beating fast in anticipation. She more resembled a boy than a mature woman who'd already borne a child.

Then he realized—she was offering herself.

It would be gentlemanly not to take advantage of her. But he was never a gentleman, and he was dying to nuzzle his face inside the wide crevice between her small breasts. Her nipples were tiny, pale pink, like cotton candy. She was born a blonde, with thin flaxen hair underneath her arms and between her legs, like on a newly hatched chicken. She was also the only decent woman he had ever had sex with. A hot head rush followed a flash of nausea. Stana's wine was returning for payback.

"Do you want me stay here with you?" she asked.

"I'm not sure."

Her chest pulsated quickly. If he waited too long, he would spoil the whole thing.

"Come closer," he said.

He propped her back against the coal barrels and put his hand under her shirt. Even smaller than it looked, her breast disappeared in his palm. He lifted her skirt and reached between her legs. She wasn't ready.

"Don't worry," she encouraged him. "I'm just a little nervous."

He wasn't ready either. What a strange day: mixing drinks, Shukri's behavior— and confronting Stana. He was useless, limp. But he needed to come. Being with a woman, however uncomfortable, always helped alleviate tension. He spat on his fingers to get her ready, moved her underwear to the side, and placed one of her legs around his waist, hoping that she hadn't tainted her shoes with manure. She was looking away, her eyes still open. With her skinny neck stretched down toward her chest she resembled a sleepy child.

The stench of ammonia from cow piss on her shoes scorched his nostrils and his eyes. The slender bones under her shirt poked him as he drew her closer. Right before he finished, he yanked himself out and splashed semen on

Mira's inner thigh. Startled by his sudden motion, Mira clamped her legs around the barrel.

The acidic wine and the taste of *rakija* filled the back of his throat and his mouth. Mira wiped his sperm off her thigh with the end of her skirt. He could still see between her legs. Her hair had grown darker. Then his stomach contracted. He bent over the manure gutter and hurled the wine with a few pieces of apple. Saliva drowned his mouth. He wiped his lips.

"You should drink some water," Mira said.

"No, I'll be okay. I just need some fresh air."

"Where are you going?"

"To Ghurge's."

"What for?"

"To have a drink."

She said nothing, but he knew she was still sitting on the barrel with her legs spread, disapproving of how much he had become like his father. At twenty-nine, a drunken old man was the only role he knew how to perform.

He stood with his back turned to her until he heard her slip off the barrel. She wrapped her arms around him and leaned her head against his back.

"You're not going to gamble, are you?" she whispered.

"Did I ever gamble?"

"We all do strange things, nowadays."

"I don't gamble."

"Can I come too?"

"No. I'm just going for a drink. Go home and pack instead. We're leaving tomorrow."

"What do you mean, leaving?"

"We have to get out of here."

"We, Halid?" Her surprise was honest. "Who's we?"

"You, me, and the boy."

"What if I don't want to go?"

"You'd rather stay here?"

"I'd rather know what you plan to do."

"You don't need to know."

"What about Stana?" she asked.

"She'll agree to anything once she gets her tractor."

"Are you sure you can do all that by tomorrow?"

"What's that supposed to mean?"

"I was just wondering how you will be able to get the tractor so quickly."

"I'll get it. Don't you worry," he said.

"Where did you plan for us to go? Sarajevo?"

"To America."

"America! Are you serious?"

"We'll discuss this in the morning." He was almost shouting, and he didn't want to shout. A ruckus would be a perfect excuse for Mother, and he didn't even dare imagine what would ensue if Stana figured out what had just gone on in her own barn.

"Halid, this can't wait." She grabbed his arm.

"In the morning, in the morning," he said as he rushed out.

10

dot burning through the blackened trees, illuminated first the contours and then the faces of the people surrounding it. The band of five men with guitars and the three drummers dictating the beat circled the fire. The music was louder than the night before. Right next to the fire a one-legged accordion player swayed from side to side, stamping his wooden foot and kicking up the dust. The stars were not out. It was close to midnight.

With their arms in the air, the Gypsy girls danced and sang between the band and the fire. Some were beautiful, their light skin almost as white as Muslim and Serbian girls. They were always the most popular among the visitors. Many found the darker ones unattractive. A particularly fair and fawnish girl caught Halid's eye. She had a white shirt on and glass jewelry over her chest, like the older Gypsy women. The light seeped through her shirt and he could see the tiny curves promising to fill into lovely breasts. How powerful youth is, he thought. Once, the magnetic power of Mira's beauty sent him into a panic. Now, after the years disarmed her, he had just left her with her legs spread over a barrel. The girl lifted her milky arms up slowly. Not over twelve, she already moved like a woman.

The barrack door was open, and he could see the heavy smoke inside. A hunch told him that Shukri already had the game going. The table was a mess, cards and money everywhere, the ring of onlookers tight around the players.

As soon as Halid entered through the barrack door, Ghurge gestured to a girl holding a tray with a pitcher. Halid took a whole pitcher and tipped the girl a five.

"Thirsty?" Ghurge asked.

"A little."

"Where were you?" Ghurge asked.

"Walking around."

"Around what? The Milosnic house?"

"What difference does it make to you?"

"Do you want to join us?" Ghurge asked.

He emptied half a pitcher and checked out the table. They were almost at the end of the hand.

"Not really."

Shukri kept his nose down.

"Are you scared?" Ghurge asked.

"Oh, shut up!" Shukri said. "He's a great player."

"Oh, you remembered me," Halid said. "Your old friend."

Shukri cringed.

"Maybe you think he'd beat me?" Ghurge mocked Shukri. "And being the kind men that you both are, you want to show pity to the old *Ciganchina*, huh?"

"Shut up, you asshole," Halid said. The beer had drowned the flutters in his stomach and spread warmth and comfort throughout his body. He could handle Ghurge without Shukri's assistance and without blowing up. "Who do you think you're fooling with this *Ciganchina* business. A fucking half-breed. Your father was a Serb."

"So what? What do you care?" The gold tooth in Ghurge's mouth sparkled. "You're just trying to get out of playing. My father doesn't mean shit to you. Half Serb or not, I am still a *Ciganchina* to all of you. Right?"

"You're not marrying my daughter," Simo said, and both he and Ghurge laughed.

"Well, with her good looks and breeding," Ghurge said, "all I could do is use her as a scarecrow. That is if the fucking government would ever let a *Ciganchina* buy any land."

"Watch yourself," Simo said and touched his gun.

"You all watch yourself in here." Ghurge spit on the floor. "My sons may have gone for the next shipment, but they'll be back any minute. Dark or not, we are a big family."

"Since when do I have to be afraid of *Cigani*?" Simo laughed.

"Since your latest glorious war efforts," Ghurge mocked right back.

Simo's elastic white fingers turned pinkish from tightening the grip on his revolver.

"All right! Let's not start any shit before we're drunk enough to start it," Shukri interrupted. "Everybody shut up." He looked at Halid. "Are you playing or not?"

Everybody in the room paused, waiting for his answer. Lale pushed through the crowd and stood behind Ghurge's chair. If Halid rejected Ghurge's challenge, he risked being seen as a coward. Being a murderer might lose him some respect, but being a coward might cost him his neck.

"I'll play a hand or two," he said.

"Now you're talking." Ghurge slapped the table in approval.

Halid turned his chair around and straddled it as he sat down to stop Ghurge's whores from sitting in his lap and peeking into his hand. That was the first lesson he learned from Father: "Never mix pussy with gambling. You can only control one at a time." An expert in the art of gambling, Father insisted he should teach Halid his best moves, "from one man to the other—the real family tradition." Halid stubbornly refused. And he kept his firm resolve even through the first year of fighting. Then, during the second year, word arrived that Father's heart had given out and he had been buried without his son's presence. Halid shuffled the deck and tried out one of the tricks he had seen Father perform. By the end of the war, he was playing every day.

He reached for his Luger and felt the leftover apple in his pocket.

Ghurge pushed the deck toward him. "Here. Deal."

HE WON THE FIRST TWO HANDS, EFFORTLESSLY, WITH A full house and three sevens, and piled maybe two or three hundred marks before him. With a little more luck he might win enough for the tractor. He had a habit of memorizing, not counting, his winnings in front of his opponents. The pitcher before him was empty and his head blurry again. The game was dragging. Ghurge had several more drinks and, judging by the color spreading over his cheeks, seemed to be getting drunker. Simo was a rotten player, did everything wrong, and paid more attention to the women around him than to the game.

The air in the barrack was stifling. Halid wasn't accustomed to playing at a table surrounded by such a big audience. During a cease-fire, when the soldiers had a chance to throw a hand or two, there was always a breeze in the trenches to clear his head. Except in July, when to ease the heat, soldiers took their boots off, ignoring the "Absolutely no bare feet when on duty!" signs posted everywhere. Even the most torturous, most tear-teasing sharp stench of un-washed socks was better than getting cooked inside the un-yielding rawhide boots. Besides, if one was unlucky enough to be stuck with a bastard rule-enforcing sergeant, there was always plenty of illegal *rakija* around to smooth things over, especially in good weather when the smugglers slipped unno-ticed behind the enemy lines.

When they were out of cash, which was more often than not—most money went for Marlboros and *rakija*—they bet a foot bath. Those who lost had to crawl to the water barrels and wash their feet and underarms under the watchful eyes of the Serbian snipers.

That was when he saw the colonel's daughter for the first time: down on his hands and knees, keeping his head as low to the ground as possible, on his way to make good on a bet. She pranced by him, the most gorgeous young thing he had ever seen, careless of the snipers, with her turquoise scarf floating about her.

"Hey dreamer! Cut already." Ghurge slammed the deck in front of him.

No big money would be made at this table. It was time to get out of the game. The best way was to lose a hand on purpose.

He waited for everybody to look at their cards, slowly sip-ping from his next pitcher. If he suddenly became hasty, the others could become suspicious and his intentions would be found out. "Always be cool," Father told him. He carefully studied Ghurge for a reaction to his hand. There was a familiarly colored shirt near Ghurge, and the effects of beer kept Halid from connecting it to any particular face until he looked up and saw Mira wearing Momir's old soccer jersey, with her hands on Lale's shoulders.

"I'm out," Shukri said, and got off the chair to greet her. She whispered something into Shukri's ear that shot a sting of jealousy through Halid.

"Well, well, look at that," he sneered. "Such good friends."

"How about you?" Ghurge asked Halid. "Or did she manage to distract you as well?"

"What was that?" Shukri asked Ghurge.

"How well you fit Momir's shoes," Halid said. "Young Shukri, protecting Mira's honor from a *Ciganchina*'s insults. Romantic. No," he answered Ghurge, "she didn't distract me. I know better."

Everybody laughed except Shukri. Mira's and Halid's eyes met. Like father, like son, she was saying. So what, he glared back boldly, he had a right to be there, and no woman would tell him where he could or could not be.

He checked his cards. Three fives. A damn good hand. There was almost a thousand on the pile. If he won the next hand, he'd be able to gather enough money for a smaller tractor. He looked at the other two cards. Two eights. Even better.

"I call five hundred," he said, and took another long sip. Ghurge accepted. Simo folded, dropping his cards on the table.

"Halid, can I talk to you outside?" Shukri asked.

Afraid for his own neck, Halid thought. If a *Ciganchina* could beat me, he could be next. He looked at Shukri's pleading face.

"Sit down and watch!" he said.

"Halid, please." Mira was ready to cry.

"Three hundred," he called.

"Two more," Ghurge answered.

Halid took the apple out. It had browned completely. He shaved the brown parts off with his teeth, spat it on the floor, and took a bite from the healthy part. The taste of the apple filled his mouth with acidic saliva before he had a chance to swallow. He took one sip of the beer, gargled, and spat the rest of the apple on the ground.

"Nothing like a homegrown Red Delicious," he said.

Ghurge had only a ten left. Halid had been counting his winnings. The man's strategy changed depending on how much money he had in his pockets and how big the pile was before him. This was an impressive pile, and his money was scarce. The last twenty Ghurge threw on the pile was all creased as if someone had made a paper boat out of it a few times. It hadn't circled the table previously, and Halid suspected it was Ghurge's lucky charm saved for the last round.

"I'll raise you another twenty." Halid grinned. It was his

last bill too, but it didn't matter—he had the dark bastard by the throat.

Ghurge couldn't ask to borrow from anyone. At this point, no one would offer. He'd have to fold. With the money, Halid would be able to get the tractor and buy tickets for himself, Mira, and the boy for as far as Sarajevo. He rubbed the sticky handle on his Luger and looked at Mira defiantly.

"Quit crying, woman," he said.

"I don't have another ten." Ghurge let his cards fall on the table. Halid was about to claim his booty when Lale put the ten deutsche marks in front of Ghurge.

"Yes you do," Lale said. It was the bill Halid had given him.

Ghurge sat up straight. "Let's see what you got," he said.

Halid showed his full house.

"Motherfucker." Ghurge's face flushed with excitement. "And I thought you'd beaten me."

Ghurge unraveled three sevens and a pair of jacks.

Halid tried to smile. The jumble in his stomach returned, and the second pitcher was low. He looked up at Mira. No, no, she was saying. Ghurge hugged the pile of money before him. He took a ten, and then another ten, and gave it to Lale.

"Tomorrow when your brothers come back, we'll find you a nice gun in the storage," he said. "You've earned it."

Lale grabbed the money and ran out of the cottage, screaming, "*Balija* lost, *Balija* lost!"

"You didn't think I had it in me, did you?" Ghurge said. "A *Ciganchina* beat the master."

He proudly stomped on the ground. "I am the best *Ciganchina* around here. And you? You just lost all your money."

He thumped both hands against the table and knocked a glass and some change off. Two young children leapt for it and ended up wrestling. The women laughed. "Victory!" Ghurge hollered, as the band members carrying their instruments poured inside the barrack. Ghurge stuck a wet bill on his forehead. The pale-skinned Gypsy girl came over and peeled it off with her lips.

Ghurge yanked his gun out of his pocket.

"Play! play!" he crooned as he emptied the charger into the ceiling.

Chunks of cement clanged onto the gambling table. The fortune-teller grabbed a few and dumped them in her pan.

"Times sure have changed," Ghurge sang. "Today I dared to beat the *hajji*."

Then he leaned over to Halid. "Do you know why your father used to beat me?" he asked. "I had to let the old sponge win, so that the other *hajji* bastards, who didn't even give a shit about him, wouldn't burn my place down. Today I say, fuck you."

"Fuck you, fuck you," the children repeated.

The old witch threw her baking pan in front of Ghurge.

"Here, sister." He flung some change in the pan. She clattered the bullets, coins, and cement in front of Halid before she tossed the whole bunch in the air. Her pan had become a twirling baton marking the day a *Ciganchina* conquered the hated Muslim landowner with a measly ten deutsche marks the dumb ass gave to one of the victor's kids.

"Did you really lose everything?" Shukri asked.

Mira was standing close enough to hear the answer.

"No," he lied, and finished the *rakija* from Shukri's glass.

The music was unbearable to Halid. So were the dancing girls. There seemed to be hundreds of them, twice as many arms, with their long necks bending, their sweaty dark bodies shaking and twisting, smiling their big, already toothless smiles. Gypsies believed dentists did the work of the Devil.

He could no longer hear the music, just the rhythm, the thump, the drumbeat hitting against his stomach, like the thickest branch hitting against Stana's living room window. One girl took off her scarf and the mass of black hair fell down her shoulders. A man at a side table gave her a bill. She smiled and wrapped the scarf around his head. It slithered to the floor.

To Halid it seemed as if the scarf continued to dance on its own. It was slinking his way. No. No. Stay away. The scarf was getting closer. He sprang up and shot three times without taking the Luger out of his pocket.

Then somebody must have tripped him. He suddenly lost his balance and fell to the floor and there was a boot on his right arm and a hand on his Luger. He clutched his fingers around his gun as firmly as he could, but the boot was pressing against his scar and his whole arm throbbed. He gave in.

Two hands reached underneath his armpits and lifted him back on his feet.

"Get out of here right away," Shukri said, facing the crowd with Halid's Luger in his hand. "I'll come to the orchard to see you."

Halid grabbed his coat off the chair, a bottle of wine from another table, and left.

IT WAS RAINING HARD AND THE WIND HAD PICKED UP, flapping his torn pant leg against his thigh. The deep mud struggled for his left shoe. The sock easily slid off his foot. The oozy mud engulfed his foot.

"Halid."

She had followed him again. He turned around.

"Did you lose everything?" she asked.

"Not everything."

"Where are you going?"

"Back to the orchard."

"Shouldn't you be inside? It's getting colder."

"No, I'll go to the orchard. It'll stop raining. See." He raised his arms to the dark sky. "It's clearing up."

"I'll come with you."

They sat down on the wet grass near the Korea. The celebratory gunshots rattled the mountain night. It had grown so dark, he could see only the buckles on her shoes through the dismal downpour.

"You're missing a shoe," she said.

"I always find the deepest mud."

"Do you remember how badly it rained the first time you walked me home?" She smiled. "How we got soaked and lost our shoes in the mud?"

"Aha."

"You were in bed for weeks with a bad cold," Mira laughed. "Your mother walked by me without saying hello for weeks. She blamed me for everything even then."

She wiggled her wet hand inside of his. "I'd be glad to leave this place," she whispered.

His stomach knotted. He'd had enough lies. He rose. "I have to tell you something."

"This is not the time for confessions," she said.

"You'll want to hear this one."

"Okay," she said.

"There is no money."

"No money?"

"No. None."

"But there is enough for the tractor, right?"

She was so small, so frail compared to the vast darkness around her.

"No. I was a little short and I thought I could win the rest."

"Short?"

"Yes."

"But you told Stana?"

"I lied."

"You lied?" She hopped to her feet. "What do you mean, you lied? Who lies about a thing like that?"

"We could still go. Regardless of the tractor. I could get a job somewhere and take care of you both."

Mira's fingers disappeared into fists.

"Bastard!" she thundered. The first punch surprised him and he fell on his back.

He curled up on his side like a shrimp, covering his face with his hands. Bastard, bastard, the words alternated with the blows, first her fists, then her feet, and then her fists again. The first five or six blows had some force and were well placed. One of them hit him in the mouth. Then her chest heaved as she tried to catch her breath, and the next round was weaker. Then an open palm—she had no energy left for a fist. It took as much energy to beat as it did to be beaten.

She was panting when she stopped. He couldn't see her face. Just her beautiful buckles shining like warm silver coins. The rain had washed the mud off them and the white moon lit them up.

"Why?" she asked. "Why did you come back?"

"I came home."

"To ruin everybody?"

"I'm sorry."

"Sorry?" she repeated in disbelief, and then broke out laughing. "He's sorry," she said as if explaining to someone. "What an idiot." She kicked him again with little force. Like pushing a sack. Then she stepped away. And a second later, the darkness swallowed her.

A DROP OF BLOOD FROM HALID'S MOUTH DRIPPED ON HIS sock. The grass was still flattened where Mira had sat not two minutes ago. By the time it sprang back up, she would have forgotten him.

Now what? Barefoot to Sarajevo, avoiding the rebel stake-outs, living at one of the shelters? To eat rancid ram soup and wear somebody else's clothes? To overhear at the breakfast table how somebody froze to death the night before rather than be captured by the military police?

His stomach fluttered again. There was nothing for him here. He needed to get away. He'd leave town tomorrow, he thought as he closed his eyes.

11

COWARDICE WAS WHAT MIRA HATED MOST.
And whining. She would haul herself out of the mess Halid
had plunged her into without whining. A low bush almost
tripped her. She cursed. She would not sit in the ditch he dug
for her. From now on, no more nonsense. She would deal
with Stana herself, rough it out with her if she had to. It
wouldn't be the first time.

When she reached the dirt path that led back to her house,
she saw refugees setting up an overnight camp on the Milosnics' land. They had pulled their wagon off the dirt road into

the wheat field and hung gaslights on the outside hooks. A woman, maybe a little older than Mira, with a pregnant belly, and two men were unloading boxes. Their tent was already up. A very thin child of maybe three was playing with a dog.

Refugees are like animals, she thought. They would soil everything. This land would belong to her son someday, when the old monster finally died. It was her duty to chase these pigs off.

"Hey!" she yelled, "you better not camp here. It's a mine-field."

The woman looked at her in horror. "But the cop told us."

"Are you kidding me? The cop? Was he tall with a mustache and capri pants?"

"Yes."

"If you're stupid enough to believe a man who dresses like an idiot, maybe you should be blown to pieces. But I'm telling you, the field is packed."

The woman grabbed the child in her arms. He whimpered at his game being cut short, swinging his legs against his mother's body. That could easily burst her water, Mira thought. These were stupid people. What in the world were they dragging a dog around for? Nothing but another mouth to feed. The woman thrust the boy away from her body to protect her stomach. Mira chased the guilt away as fast as she could. Generosity was a luxury around here, and in the past it had brought nothing but misery to her.

The two men started to carefully load their handheld bundles onto their bicycles and the big boxes back into the wagon. They had aimed to stay awhile, she thought. It's a good thing she caught them in time. A few hours later and they would have grown roots. She heard dreadful stories about the stubborn refugees. They remained even after the villagers set their property on fire. Resilient, like viruses.

"Did the cop tell you that my husband was blown to pieces, right on the other side of that field?" Mira asked.

"No. Oh, my God, hurry, but be careful," the woman said to the two men. She was struggling with the boy who was sobbing and the dog that was pawing at her legs.

"Well, he did," Mira lied, angry with the boy. Her father never allowed her to keep an animal, not even when resources were not as scarce. When he found her favorite Cornish hen underneath the quilt in Mira's bed, he called it a dirty disease-carrying chicken and threw it out the bedroom window. The fall broke its leg, and the hen limped for the rest of its life.

The taller of the two men anxiously threw the last box onto the wagon. If they are not neat when they leave they will turn up all the seeds from the soil, Mira thought. The wheat may not have taken root deep enough.

"I think that this area," she said, and showed the direct line from where they were standing to the dirt path, "is the safest. Try getting to the road, as quickly as possible."

"Thank you," the woman said. "Sorry about your husband."

MIRA TIPTOED THROUGH THE FRONT GATE. THE UPSTAIRS was hushed. Usually, Stana would jiggle her hammock or drop the lighter or a plate on the floor as soon as Mira entered the house. It was the warning that the mistress was listening.

Mira stopped in front of the staircase. Another minute or two and she'd be ready. She went into the garden to check on Mladen. The door on the cage was wide open and he was sleeping.

Mira sat on the edge of a flowerpot next to the cage. He was so relaxed. The calm with which Mladen slept always tickled her. She knew nothing about peace. Her nights were always ridden with trouble.

What a strange face he has, she thought. He barely resembled anyone human. The "growing disease" had changed his features. His nose grew longer. It hung over his lips, purple from his ailing heart. Two large ball-like tumors protruded from his forehead. A monster, even to Mira, who loved him. Yet even if his body almost outgrew the cage built for him, he seemed too good to have left a girl dead with a broken neck at the river's edge.

Mladen opened his eyes.

"You must miss Momir." He got up and put his bare feet on the ground. For years now no one could find a shoe that matched his foot size. "I miss him too."

Mira rose and sat next to him.

"We have to be careful not to break the bench," he said. "I'm heavy and with you next to me, I'm even heavier."

She smiled and the tears followed. Once, as a little girl she saw him pick up a full-grown pig to entertain Momir. Mira was terrified of pigs as if she were Muslim and would keep herself as far away as she could from the ravenous sounds inside the pens. The fearlessness with which Mladen lifted the screeching animals made her feel safe. He was the only man she thought stronger than Momir.

"Are you going away?" He touched her cheek with his index finger.

"There is no money to go away with."

"Then you must convince Mother you have to stay. She's set to see you go. That's all she's been talking about."

Those were the first wise words she'd heard in this house. Even Pap had made a mistake. Mira laid her head in Mladen's lap, hoping that the tears would tire her soon. He petted her head gently.

"Why do you stay in this cage?" she asked. "You could come up, if you wanted. Your mother doesn't have to know."

"It makes the town sleep tighter when I'm in my cage."

"Did you have anything to do with that little girl dying?" She had never asked him before.

"I don't know. I don't remember. That's why it's good that I am in the cage."

"I'm done crying." She sat back up.

"Then you should go upstairs. And don't worry about waking the boy. He had a hearty dinner with me. He must be sound asleep."

"Good night." She kissed him. He blushed.

"Mira," Mladen called after her.

"Yes?"

"Be firm, if you must."

STANA WAS LYING ON HER SIDE FACING THE WINDOW. Mira stopped. If she let this drag on for too long, she'd lose. The old woman was a much tougher fighter than she. Stana was the one who withstood all the rumors that almost drowned the house; she was the one who madly fought for the preservation of their good name. Mira would rather have flung herself from the top of the Dinara than stand by the girl accused of marrying her son while pregnant with another man's child. But Stana was growing older and weaker, and Momir's death had broken her spirit. Soon she'd need someone to look after everything.

Mira turned the light on, something she wouldn't have dreamed of the day before. Stana had limited all electricity consumption in the house. Mira grabbed one end of the hammock with both hands and shook it as hard as she could.

Stana sat up, confused. A thin greenish cataract film covered her eyes. This was new to Mira. It had been almost five years since she stood this close to her mother-in-law.

"Listen," she started, before she was even sure if Stana was awake enough to understand her. "Get up."

"Get up, I said," she repeated and shook the hammock again.

"What's going on?" Stana was still in a daze.

"The boy is Momir's," Mira said. "And we are staying. End of story."

"What?" Stana propped herself up. "Like hell you are, you slut." Then she laughed. "What's the matter?" Her voice was hoarse, but her mind had cleared. "Your Muslim boy messed up? Did he lose the money like that no-good father of his?"

Mira let go of the hammock.

Stana laughed again. "You knew that he was stupid, that he was no match for Ghurge and the rest of the bastards."

Mira could never handle Stana's insight, and she backed up another step.

"Well, too bad. I guess you and your circumcised son of a bitch are just gonna have to make do with what he's got left."

If Mira didn't act now, she and her son could be thrown out of the house before the morning. There was no other choice. She tightened her fists, clenched her jaw, and took a swing as hard as she could.

"Ay," Stana cried out, covering her face with her hands.

"Listen!" Mira yelled. "Soon, you'll be bed bound. Who will look after you and Mladen. Pap? You know damn well that he'll be dead soon. So if you want me to be good to you, you better be good to me."

Stana was still holding her face. "I'd rather die," she said.

"You don't mean that. And if you did, do you want Mladen to be taken away by the government?"

"I will find a way. You're the last person I want to depend on." Stana tried to get up, but the punch must have made her light-headed; she fell back into her hammock.

"I told you you'll be needing me soon. What do you think will happen to Mladen after you're gone? How long do you think the villagers will let him live before they seek vengeance for a broken neck?"

Stana's head was down, she was weakening.

"What about Halid?" Stana asked.

"Don't you worry about him."

"He's going to want the boy."

"No, he's not."

"You're dumber than I thought," Stana said. "He's going to come tomorrow and ask for the boy."

"No, he won't. He's got nothing to come back with. Ghurge and Shukri won all of his money."

"What an ass." Stana laughed. "He may still come. Those Muslim bastards are the law now."

"He'll be too ashamed to show his face. Believe me."

"God have mercy on you both when your time comes," Stana said, in a whisper much gentler than the biting tone with which she held court in the living room earlier that morning.

"Don't you worry about God. Just make sure you do what's best for the family."

"Get out of my room, you scum," Stana said.

Outside the bedroom, trembling with adrenaline like an ambushed soldier, Mira leaned against the wall and listened for Stana's reaction. Nothing. Then she heard a sound, as if the hammock was moving, the body adjusting inside it. But it was a cautious move, nothing like the deliberate noise used to enforce fear. Then there was silence. Mira's knees gave in, and she hit the concrete floor. She had won.

12

HIS MOUTH WAS CRUSTED WITH DRIED
blood and he was shivering when he woke up with the wet
clothes glued to his body. His back was cramped and his foot
asleep from lying in the same position. It was somewhere between two and three o'clock in the morning. The dark was
unyielding—just dull black stripes instead of tree trunks, and
the sharper darkness in between. Not a sound could be heard.

The bottle of wine was empty. He felt around to see if it
spilled, but the grass was still wet from the rain. He tasted the
blades next to the bottle. Nothing. Not a drop.

He coiled his back, trying to get more comfortable, and saw a fire in the ravine, six, seven hundred yards away. The fire must be warm, he thought. It would be wonderful to be dry, have a drink, eat.

The cold bit the skin through his torn pant leg. He tried getting up, but his body was too sore, too drunk to stand up. He rolled over onto all fours and tried crawling.

The pebbles on the ground hurt his cold palms and his exposed knee, but that pain was more tolerable than the one ravaging his back. The naked patches of soil were muddy, and his knee sank in. The mud was warmer than the windy air and not at all unpleasant. During summertime, he used to love burying himself in the warm clay mud.

The ground beneath him changed as he inched forward, and now the wet grass rubbed his knee. He was accustomed to creeping through the trenches, over sand, gravel, and concrete, even over bodies, but it wasn't wartime anymore. The cuddling of the chilly blades surprised him. It was like soft ice.

He had almost five hundred yards left to the flame. He licked a few drops off a low-hanging branch and continued. The pale yellow flame was blue in the middle. Nothing like the beast of a campfire earlier in the Korea. This one was more like the candle flames he saw at the Christian Orthodox services. The candles were melted beeswax shaped like hives. He could hear the fire flicker. It would be nice to fall asleep listening to the logs snapping.

He was near the fire now and he could discern the faces:

Shukri, Ghurge, Rade, and Simo. Ghurge grabbed the rifle and peered in his direction. Halid ducked to the ground. Better be careful. They might think he was a rabid raccoon or a squirrel. Only sick animals crept near the fire this close to the village.

"We got mouths to feed," Shukri said.

"True," Ghurge agreed.

"So what do we do?" The veins on Shukri's temples popped out. He inhaled the cigarette smoke meditatively. "Wait for the government or do it ourselves?"

"The government?" Simo scoffed and booted the kindling. "They haven't paid the police or the army for months. They've got the big-city smart mouths to worry about first. The villagers come last."

"You're right," Ghurge agreed. "My pension hasn't arrived in almost a year. My kids are hungry."

"Oh, shut up!" Shukri said. "Your kids are not hungry."

"Calm down, both of you." Rade was impatient. "The point is, we'd do better things with Halid's money than he. He already gambled half of it away."

Halid squeezed a rock in his hand. A lot more than half.

"We owe it to Colonel Mashan," Rade said.

"Yeah, he led our soldiers to victory," Ghurge agreed.

"Oh, shut up," Shukri barked at Ghurge. "What do you care about our soldiers? You sold as many guns to the Serbs as you did to Muslims."

"But I charged them more."

Simo and Rade burst out laughing.

"You are such an idiot," Shukri said.

"The truth is, Colonel Mashan is returning soon. The town is preparing the welcoming party and we're playing cards with the perpetrator who shot his daughter. That can't be good for anybody's business," Simo said.

"What took you so long to tell us?" Ghurge asked Shukri.

"Tell the dirty Gypsy not to speak to me," Shukri said to Simo.

"Let's talk about something else," Ghurge suggested. "What are we going to do if there's an investigation?"

"Who's going to investigate? Me?" Simo ridiculed him.

"Should we tell Pap?" Rade asked.

"No. First of all, he'd never agree to it, especially not for his golden boy," Shukri said.

"But if it's going to be the town's decision, and the money is going to benefit all of us, then he should understand," Rade said.

"And if he doesn't?" Shukri asked.

"Then he doesn't know what's best for him," Simo said.

"I say we leave Pap out. He's too old to matter, but he has a lot of friends. Imagine! If the women make noise, we'd end up with an outside investigation."

"Women always make noise, and it doesn't amount to anything unless the men raise their knives. Leave the women to me," Shukri said.

"All of them?" Ghurge mocked. "I bet you'd like that."

"I won't stand for a smutty *Ciganchina* talking about decent women." Shukri stood up to leave.

"He's right," Simo told Ghurge scornfully. "You just sit there and let us talk. We'll tell you what to do. Now, if there is a federal investigation, I'll take care of it. I'll make back entries in my journal recording Halid's violent outbursts. We have witnesses for last night's shooting. Even if they send someone, which I doubt, the Vejzagic family has no muscle around here anymore, and they'll rule self-defense."

"Will Gypsies testify?" Rade asked.

"They will if I ask them," Ghurge said.

"You should write those notes anyway," Rade said. "In case some respectable city Muslims decide to come sniffing around."

"Sure."

"Are we all set?" Rade asked.

"No guns, remember," Shukri said.

"Fine. When?"

"Tomorrow, early," Shukri said. "I know where he sleeps."

Shukri and Rade shook hands over the flame. Halid wished they'd burn themselves. The plan was excellent, he had to agree. He'd made a sufficient menace of himself to justify what they were doing. His cheeks were burning and the flutters in his stomach were swelling, pushing all the way up his throat. He had to breathe slowly to keep from throwing up. It was so tempting to let out a howl and let them know he was there.

All four men were ready to leave.

A strange sensation passed through his body, a heat wave, an electrical wave, like when he was on guard and didn't know from which direction the sniper fire would come. He couldn't help but agree: he was guilty. The image of the girl returned, so exquisite, so refined, even in her death, a prized nugget. An innocent accident, just like the wallet he stumbled on in her pocket. He was trying to button her coat to keep her warm when he rubbed against something, like a loaf of bread, in her pocket. He was hungry, but it was a man's wallet. He opened it and counted the money in disbelief. Almost two thousand. A fortune. He clutched the bills with his teeth as he soaked in the river. He intended to keep quiet. And then, a few days later he was gambling like a rich Russian before the Revolution: burning with spending fever.

A terrible cramp shot up his legs. He rose and rushed toward the orchard, ignoring the branches scratching against his skin until he hurt so badly he was forced to slow down. Then the shapes of trees, the long bush formations, the large protruding rocks, all looked unfamiliar. The army training had taught him to measure distance without instruments by calculating his pace and the time elapsed, and yet he was lost.

Momir would have sniffed his way back home from miles away, like a cat. Then why, why didn't he smell out the powder buried inside the plastic shell of a land mine? He thought of Momir blowing up, legs first, then arms catching fire, spreading slowly toward the middle of his body, his guts—the sight he feared most. It was easy to die quickly, in a flash.

A branch broke under someone's foot. Unexpected company. He strained to see past the trees. There was a small bulge next to one of the trunks. Holding the bush branches to stop them from swooshing, he started to retreat. Then he recognized a crooked poplar. The orchard was but a few hundred yards away. He was in his own territory. As soon as he reached the dirt road, he dove into the drainage ditch on the side and lay as low as he could.

A slouched figure scurried by several moments later. Then it stopped.

"Halid?" the low voice called. "Is that you?"

It was Mother.

He stumbled out, embarrassed. After five years of separation, she saw him first inside a mud-filled hole.

"Son. They're planning to kill you." She approached him with urgency.

He wiped his dirty hands on his pants, then realized he had only one shoe.

"How are you?" he asked.

"Did you hear what I said?" She walked over to him. "They're planning to kill you. We must do something. One of Ghurge's daughters came by to warn me."

She was half the size she was when last he saw her—and still she tried to protect him.

"Why are you out in this cold?" he asked.

She grabbed him by both arms. "Did you hear me? We have to do something!"

"You can't help." His lungs were burning. "Go away, please. I have to think of something myself."

"I can't. You're my son." There were tears on her face.

"Do you have any weapons left?"

"No. The Serbs robbed the last stash, and I gave the bullets I had in the house to our soldiers."

"How about a knife?"

"Just some dull, useless kitchen utensils."

"Then there is nothing you can do. Nothing. You should go home."

She picked up a bundle off the ground she must have dropped when she saw him.

"I brought you some clean clothes," she said. "They may be too big for you now. You're so thin."

It was his good white linen suit he saved for weddings and similar occasions, and Father's presentable pair of shoes.

"Why are these still around?" he asked about the shoes.

"We buried him in his old pair," she said.

"You shouldn't have done that."

"When you're dead, you don't care much."

He took the fragrant bundle from her hands. "Thank you for your kindness, Mother."

The suit was carefully folded. Mother starched it herself each time she washed it and folded mothballs inside to make sure it didn't get eaten. Halid had left the suit at the bottom of his trunk the day he packed for war.

"Come home, son."

She touched him before he had a chance to draw back, and her hand lingered on his arm longer than he thought necessary.

"I can't."

"Is that where you were shot?" she asked.

"Yes."

"Does it hurt?" She caressed it.

"No. Don't." Her gentle touch felt as if the flesh was torn all over again by the burning metal.

"Don't you care that they want to kill you?"

He didn't answer.

"Please come home with me," she said.

"What home? To the little run-down shack?"

They were the last house in the village to give up using an outhouse—in '87, two years after the last, most impoverished Christians.

"It's still our home. Let's go."

"I can't," he said.

"Why?"

"I just can't."

"What happened to you while you were away, son?"

"It's time for you to go."

"Tell me, please, son," she said. "Get it off your chest. Whatever it is, Allah will forgive."

"Allah, Mother?"

"He knows that you're not a bad man like your father was. He doesn't want you to pay for his sins."

"What do you know about sins?"

"Plenty. Everybody does. Everybody does bad things. Father was bad, but you're not. You're just his child."

"Father wasn't a bad man. He was a drunk."

"He was more than just a drunk. He was a gambler, a coward, a liar, and the worst kind of husband possible. But you are nothing like him."

It must have been hell to be Father's wife. To a poor fifteen-year-old, who was not yet menstruating, being the bride of a landowner's only son must have sounded so promising. Grandfather paid five milking cows and an ox for his son's new bride. The day of the wedding she wore twenty golden ducats around her temples for everyone to see that no expenses were spared on the day the *bey* married his son.

"Why don't you come home with me?" She sensed his melting. "We can pay whatever you owe. That is . . ." She was caught meddling, and ashamed, she looked away. "If you owe anything to anyone. Son, we've got plenty of land left."

"It's all bad."

"It won't always be."

"Mother, I need to think right now. Alone. And you shouldn't be out in this cold."

"You are what's important now."

"Mother! Listen. You have to go," he said. "If you don't go, I will. If it makes you feel better, I'll go find Pap, see if he can think me out of this one. But there is nothing you can take care of. This is my business. Understand?"

She covered her face with her hands. "Allah Hue Giber. Allah Hue Giber."

He couldn't bear the sight of her shriveled hands covered with dark purple patches and the crooked fingernails turned yellow from smoke.

"No." He moved her hands away from her face. "Please don't!"

She bent down on the ground in the praying position.

He grabbed her by the shoulders and forced her up. "Goddamn it, woman, leave me!" Halid recited the words Father would stammer as he struggled with Mother at the front door when he returned from the tavern at night. She'd provoke him to hit her rather than let him trash the house. A little bruise here and there was nothing, she'd say. The broken glasses and plates cost money.

"There is nothing of him in you. He was a sick drunken fool."

"So am I, Mother, so am I."

"No, you're not," she said. "Maybe a little now because of the war, but that is normal."

"Really? Remember the *rakija* barrel you distilled to sell? Father finished it in two nights. I could do it in one."

"I don't believe you. You couldn't be just like your father. You are my son too."

"I am worse than he was, Mother. I am a murderer."

"Don't say that, son," she whispered. "It was the war."

"I killed an innocent girl, Mother. Colonel Mashan's beautiful daughter. More beautiful even than Mira was when she was young."

"Things like that happen in war."

"There was no fighting going on."

"Then it must have been an accident."

"I robbed her, Mother, and I lied to everyone."

"Son," she said quietly, "all I want is for you to come home. We can forget about the past together."

"Maybe you can, but not me."

"Please, come home," she murmured and collapsed on the ground.

He was tired too. And afraid. Afraid that she would recuperate in a minute, get up, touch him, and plead some more for him to please, please be a good son and come home. He couldn't cross over that doorstep, look inside the living room, at the old linen chest where she hid his allowance from Father, underneath the folded holiday table spread.

"Go back to your embroidery, Mother," he said. "You can't save me."

And before he'd have to endure the sound of her crying anymore, he walked away as fast as he could, welcoming the sting of branches against his face. He bit through his lip until it bled, and when he saw the metal reflection of the moon taking its bath in the stream, he plunged his face into the freezing water and let it burn, burn, until it burned so much that the voice of his mother, his mother he left in the orchard, finally stopped whispering in his ear—come home, come home, come home.

13

THE MOON WAS THINNING AND WHITENING and the deep pink of a new day bled through the wall of reeds lining the stream. The clouds, where the night still hovered, were dark purple and brown. Soon it would dawn. It was the sleepiest time of the night, the time when soldiers fell asleep on guard, causing their troops to be caught and slaughtered in the predawn slumber. If he was to defend himself against his attackers, he needed to be awake and alert.

He took his clothes off and sat down on the clay bank, letting the water run over his legs. The murky water sped by and he couldn't see his feet, couldn't move them. By now, his toes had probably turned blue. He lifted his legs out. His toenails were iridescent, like the stomach of a young trout pulled out of the water at night, all speckled with red and turquoise.

He slapped his left foot. The slap burned badly. The shivers from his toes inched up his spine, all the way to his neck seeking warm skin to feed on, as if he was curled up back inside the trench fighting a storm, wet to the bones, as soldiers called it. Wetter than the rain itself, they said, without any chance of drying again.

He forced his eyes to stay open. It was dangerous to close them right before dawn. "That's when the ghosts get you," a young man Halid met at the infirmary told him. "They inhabit the place inside your eyelids, and if you're careless and fall asleep, they come, and you're finished." The young man was the only survivor of a grisly stakeout. The massacre claimed his entire family and left him with the worst case of insomnia in the ward's history. When the young man's weary body finally surrendered several weeks later, Halid hoped that it wasn't the ghosts that brought about the tender creature's meeting with the rest of his folk.

Halid smelled himself. The sweat had hardened the hair underneath his armpits. It itched and he still stank. He should wash and change. If he wore his best, he'd have more clout in negotiating. He jumped, shrugging the sleepiness off his shoulders.

THE WHITE SUIT GLOWED IN THE MOONLIGHT EXACTLY
where he left it. An encouraging omen. He dropped to his
knees and picked it up carefully, like a precious relic.

As if he were performing the first *rak'a* of the dawn prayer,
he immersed his hand in the water and washed behind his
ears as the K'uran ordered. "Bismillahhir rahmanir rahim,"
he recited, sure that he was doing it all wrong.

Those were the only three words of prayer he knew for
sure. Most of his generation never learned any before they
were shot and brought to the hospital. There, the most persuasive, charming, and seductive mullahs floated from one
bed to the other and offered the wisdom of the Koran, an
expensive-looking leather-bound book that read backwards
in a language nobody understood.

They paid special attention to those left in the corridor,
those who would soon die and were removed from the room
so as not to dampen the spirits of the others. If death was expected that day, the mullah stayed on his knees chanting side
by side with the inconsolable friends and family members.

Some soldiers dragged their beds close to the door to listen to the foreign words. Some even believed that if they
closed their eyes to the sound of the *sura*, they would be protected from the eye-dwelling ghosts. Halid stayed away, but
he could not help occasionally letting the powerful sounds
steal his attention and lull him to rest.

The skin under his armpits was warm and it scorched his freezing fingers. "Elemtere keyfe feaale rabbuke bi eshabil fil. Elem yecaal . . ." He dressed slowly, deliberately, the way the martyrs do before sacrifice. If somebody saw him now, they would have no right to think him mad.

BY NOW, THE RED SUNLIGHT HAD CONQUERED THE SKY, except a few plum-colored patches where clouds held on. He would go to Pap first. He crossed the bridge over the stream and hiked up the mountain toward Pap's house. When he arrived, he found the house dark and the shutters down. He could hide inside while Pap talked to Shukri. There was no answer. If he broke the window, the shattered glass would betray him.

The paling quarter moon was almost invisible. The early sunshine threw its rays over the ravine and burned up the rest of the clouds, promising to bring a beautiful day. The cool daybreak air caressed his ears, his neck, his chest.

The Dinara's biggest boulder, turning from silver to gold, dominated the skyline. Underneath it, the cliffs sloped gently toward the village. The bushes, the rocks, and the trees around him were taking their daytime color. He scanned the small roofs on top of other small roofs of the distant villages and the contours of the nearest houses and barns. He realized soon he'd be noticeable from afar.

"Momir!" he yelled. "You dumb bastard, why didn't you

watch where you were going?" The circling wind picked up the sound and carried it across the ravine.

The echo didn't bounce back. There would be no answers for Halid. Fortune favored the brave, not the cowardly.

Shukri, he remembered. He could talk to Shukri. They were always friends. Then he remembered the song Father owed Shukri.

"TONIGHT MY HEART SUFFERS!" he shouted.

"NITE-ART-FFERS," the echo moaned, followed by the dogs' barking.

"Now Shukri can hear the payback.

"SHUKRI," he bellowed.

"KRI," the mountain hollered back. The dogs howled.

"WE ARE EVEN."

"VEN," the echo responded, the dogs going crazy.

He had settled his father's last bill. Now he was ready for a fight.

THE LAST CROWING OF THE COCKS CAUGHT HIM NEARING Shukri's house somewhere between four thirty and five o'clock. The house was smaller than Mother's but in far better shape. Not only had Shukri come back from Sarajevo months before Halid, but his younger brother stayed back on account of his bad eyes and tended the farm during the war. Shukri was married and there were traces of a hardworking woman all around the front door. The flowerpots were watered, the doormat shaken of dust and mud, and the few pairs of shoes deposited on the shoe shelf were freshly polished. Halid knocked carefully.

There was no answer.

He knocked again, louder this time, thinking of the times when the idea of knocking at Shukri's door would seem ridiculous. Unlike at Momir's, where Stana's stern presence scared the boys away, at Shukri's, Halid and Momir would kick off their shoes, leap over the doorstep, and wait around the kitchen for Shukri's mother to give them some bread and sugar, which was their bribe for taking Shukri's younger brother along. Shukri was ashamed of his brother's poor sight and always ignored him wherever they went. Momir and Halid liked Smail and would challenge anyone who would dare to call him "ashtray eyes," mocking the size of his glasses.

A voice answered, "Who is it?"

"Halid."

There was a quiet commotion behind the door. He heard voices. Then the door opened.

Like Shukri's mother, his wife was mild tempered. Despite her early marriage to Shukri—she was brought over at sixteen—she found happiness in her good-natured mother-in-law and a brother-in-law who had become a master farmer. The three of them spent most of their time looking after the farm and Shukri's two children.

"Is your husband home?" Halid asked.

"He's still asleep. So are my kids." Her reply was fast and rehearsed. She had been instructed on what to say.

177

"Where are his boots?" Halid pointed at the shelf.

"I took them in for cleaning." Her cheeks flushed.

"How long has he been sleeping?"

"He got home a couple of hours ago. He hasn't been home for nearly two days. But I'm sure you know that. You want me to wake him?"

"Would you?"

"Come on in and wait in the kitchen."

The kitchen was the first room of the three. It had a nice dining room table Halid didn't remember with four chairs. A vase was in the middle on a knitted cloth. All over the room he noticed the hand of a good wife. A bundle of newspapers on one side of the table seemed oddly out of place, as if thrown there in a hurry. Underneath it, a knife handle peeked out. Halid recognized the carving on the handle. It was Momir's old *chakija*. He had lost it in a bet with Shukri.

Shukri appeared wearing the same pants as the night before, with messy hair, and he was naked above the waist. His boots were on, laced all the way up and dirty.

"Your wife must've been reading the paper when I knocked," Halid said.

"She must have." Shukri walked to the table and straightened the paper. "What brings you to my house?" he asked.

"I wanted to make sure you heard my song."

"That was you?" Shukri smiled.

"You said my father owed you a song."

"It was a joke."

"A debt is no joke."

"True."

"So, are we even?" Halid said. "Do you release me from my debts?"

Shukri looked away.

"I'm asking seriously."

"I don't know, Halid. You've done a lot of damage around here."

"It can be repaired."

"I'm not so sure. The best thing for you would be to leave. Leave right away."

Their eyes met. Shukri was staunch—no mercy, no negotiation.

"I'll leave. But I have a favor to ask."

"What is it?"

"If anything should happen to me, promise me that Mother and Mira will have enough to get by. That you will take care of them," Halid said.

Shukri shifted his weight from one leg to the other. "I always have."

"Do I have your word?" Halid asked.

"When did you ever need it?"

"I do now," Halid said.

"Then you have my word. Is that all?"

"Yes. Thank you."

The door closed behind him without a sound.

THE RADIANT DAWN BLEW IN ON A GENTLE BREEZE. THE trees with their few remaining leaves soaked up the mild October sun, as if they knew they would soon be surrounded by low gray skies and the thick smell of November. The field of dry cornstalks whirred in the wind, waiting to be chopped down so next year's crop could be planted. Corncobs were Halid's favorite pretend guns when he was growing up. The sparrows chirped, bathing in the drying potholes. They would be plunging to their deaths half-frozen off the telephone wire not three months ahead.

Pap and Halid once built a birdhouse where they would put some wheat for the birds to eat. The village's poorest mothers sent their children to steal the wheat—the winter wasn't harsh on only the birds.

THE TOWN WAS STILL ASLEEP. IT ALL SEEMED LESS threatening in the quiet: the smatterings of bombed buildings, the dug-up roads, the scorched and caved roofs. The river gurgled loudly, unobstructed by the noises of the day. Across the street from Rade's bakery, the new tenants in the abandoned house were hanging the laundry. They used black garbage bags to cover the broken windows, except for one, which they covered in bright-colored plastic, probably for a child's room. The woman was tall and plump. The man was broad shouldered and red faced. He looked like someone who never yelled and who drank a little beer before going to bed—just enough for a good night's sleep. Sturdy folk. A child ran down the stairs wearing a pair of cleats and chasing a leather soccer ball. They would prosper, he was sure.

He entered the bakery.

"Rade," he called.

Rade came out with a pan of bread in his arms.

"Halid?" He was more reluctant and scared than a man who had just been interrupted from sliding a pan of bread dough inside the oven should be. He wasn't expecting Halid.

"Are you surprised to see me?" Halid asked.

"No."

"Then why are you so nervous?"

"I'm not. What brings you to my store so early?"

"I had a question for you. Did my old man owe you anything?" Halid asked.

Rade looked at him suspiciously.

"Did he?"

"No."

"Sure?"

"What's gotten into you since you came back?" Rade asked. "You don't seem like yourself."

"It's a beautiful day." Halid pointed outside the store window. "I wanted to make sure that on a day like this nobody has a bad thing to say about my father."

"He owed me nothing."

"That's good," Halid said.

"I always liked your father," Rade said.

"Really?" Halid leaned over the counter, knocking over the two loads of bread and wrapping paper. "What about me?"

Rade backed off.

"Did you ever like me?" Halid repeated.

"Halid, why don't you sit down?"

"No." Halid stepped on the wrapping paper. "I have to head back home."

"So you're going to see your mother?"

"Maybe."

The door rang again and a Gypsy girl came in with a child in her arms. She wasn't over fifteen years old and the baby hung haphazardly on her arm. She smiled at Rade.

"Got some extra bread for me now?"

"Didn't I tell you to come back later?" Rade said.

"We are hungry now."

"Is that boy yours?" Halid asked Rade, and the girl laughed.

"Who's this?" she asked.

"A soldier friend."

"The rabid one? The one Ghurge beat last night?"

"Don't you have somewhere else to go?" Rade yelled at the girl.

"No, not really. The empty belly makes it difficult to go anywhere."

"Here." Halid took three bread loaves off the counter and handed them to the girl. "For your kid."

"My God," she said.

"And don't eat it all at once."

"I won't."

Rade was furious, but he said nothing. Halid turned his back to both of them and left the store.

THE MINARET ON THE NEWLY RENOVATED MOSQUE WAS glowing in the sunshine. The grass around the ancient turbaned graves was manicured. Despite the summer drought, it looked fresh and green. During Halid's childhood, it was against an unspoken law to try to maintain any religious temples.

On the mosque porch there were at least three hundred pairs of worn-out shoes. A lot of men were praying inside. He couldn't recall if he ever saw more than a dozen pairs growing up. Nobody used to pray. He walked up to the porch, grabbed an armful of shoes, and hurled them into the air. They landed silently in the grass like acorns after a strong wind. They were beautiful lying like that, some with their soles up, some on the side, like good women peacefully sleeping. A young boy ran inside the mosque screaming "Thief, thief." Seconds later several grown men rushed out to the street in their bare feet. He knew a few faces. They were boys when he left. Now they were men, respectable men witnessing another gone mad.

"Crazy," one of them yelled.

He turned the corner onto the main street. The children tailed.

"Soldier's crazy. Soldier's crazy."

Most of the shops hadn't opened yet, except for the cigarette stand. The goldsmith's widow, Saliha, stood outside her store underneath the awning. She blew a kiss toward the sky and pressed her hand across the front of her brown sheepskin vest when she saw him.

"Halid!" She ran across the road with a bag in one hand. "Thank God I saw you. My dreams came back last night. I saw the murderers over my husband's dead body. Shukri, Rade, and the dark one. They mean to do the same to you."

"I know."

"Here." She unwrapped a butcher knife from its leather cover. "I heard they stole your gun. Cut them up well. I'll gut them for the dogs."

"I will."

He watched as Saliha disappeared inside her stand and waited until she snapped the padlock shut.

The barefoot crowd of men, with women in tow, quickly swelled. Several men had obviously dressed in a hurry, wearing pajama bottoms or wool underpants and sweaters. The women were in housedresses with their hair covered with scarves. Then a few more young children ran out of the schoolyard, followed by two happy strays.

"Crazy! Crazy," they were chanting.

As Halid passed the pile of abandoned cars he saw another crowd stationed along the road as if a circus parade were passing by. Several hundred yards ahead, next to the fountain festooned with more curious onlookers, he saw Ghurge and Simo armed with sharp knives and firm resolve. Two women were holding Mother. She was squealing, and her shrill cries silenced the rhythmic chants behind him. The town went mute. Ghurge motioned the followers to halt. Rade pushed through the people with a small curved *chakija* in his hands. Panting, he probably had to run around in a big loop to end up facing Halid.

"Shame on you. He's alone," a voice screamed from a balcony. Halid searched for its source, but the tight circle now surrounding him obstructed his vision.

The three men stepped forward and moved to surround him. Rade was pale and his apron was wrinkled, a huge contrast to Simo's immaculate uniform. Ghurge looked exactly the same as always.

"Watch out, he's got a knife," someone behind him yelled. Halid spun around quickly and saw Shukri. The sun was right behind him, but he could still see the flash of metal in Shukri's hand.

"So, you're going to kill me," Halid said. "And with Momir's *chakija*."

Shukri froze.

"Shukri, please," Mother cried.

Halid swung his head from one side to the other so that he

could keep his eyes on all four men at the same time. Shukri wouldn't strike first. Maybe Rade wouldn't either.

"What are you guys waiting for?" Simo asked.

Shukri looked at Simo as if he was surprised to see him. Good, Halid thought. He's having second thoughts.

"Shukri, brother," he said. "Don't let him do this."

"Come on," Simo said.

Ghurge drew closer. Halid sensed him, swerved around, and stabbed him in the shoulder. Then an unbelievable pain tore through his back: Simo.

"Oh God," he heard himself scream.

Halid fell down to his knees and grabbed his back. His palm was stained with blood. Rade kicked the knife out of his hand.

"Is this what you want?" He showed his blood to Shukri.

Shukri looked away again.

Then Simo approached him from the front, his face on fire, his eyes glazed with the same wrath Halid saw in his platoon members before they slit their prisoners' throats.

Halid tried to get up. The sharp pain shot down his leg. The knife was still in his back. He pushed as hard as he could. A little more. There. He was standing.

Suddenly Ghurge was in front of him. There was another sharp pain cutting through the front of his stomach. Then Ghurge stepped away, yanking the knife out. Halid looked down at his body. His white pants were red. Another sharp pain shot through his stomach, and Halid grabbed it with both hands, afraid that he might lose something in all this warm pouring blood.

He fell down to his knees. Then he realized that he was dying, and panic overwhelmed him. He tried to force himself up, tried to order his legs, get up, get up. The harder he pushed his palms and his feet into the ground, the more difficult it was to stay kneeling. He fell on his side.

Above him a vast sky. Blue, blue, and more blue. Then he saw Father at the riverbank. He was pulling the fishing net out of the water.

"Halid," Father yelled excitedly. "Come help me pull the bait out of his mouth. He is holding on too tight, the bastard."

Then he saw Shukri leaning over him with Mother behind his shoulder. Her mouth was open like a fish, with no sound.

"Is he dead?" Simo asked.

Not yet. He didn't want to die looking at their faces, so he rolled toward the old poplar that grew behind the fountain. A cardinal had landed on the branch and started to sing.

He was glad it was a cardinal. He couldn't stand to hear anything blue.

Then there was a kick in his back, but it was dull and didn't hurt. Then there were gentle hands and a sound, son, son, son in his ear. He tried to say something but his mouth was filled with fluid.

He was choking in blood, he realized. Well, ancestors, unlike Father, I have followed the family tradition.

HOMECOMING

Natasha Radojčić

A READER'S GUIDE

To print out copies of this or other
Random House Reader's Guides,
visit us at www.atrandom.com/rgg

Questions for Discussion

1. Radojčić titles her book *Homecoming*, and yet Halid never actually returns to his childhood home. In chapter one, he gets off the bus and thinks, "home, the last place in the world he wanted to see." Why does Halid resist going home? How has he changed? Besides war, what other life events—traumatic or otherwise—can become points of no return? What would life look like without any such events?

2. This novel has been praised for its searing effect upon readers. A critic remarked that *Homecoming* offered "something rarely seen in contemporary fiction: a tragedy." Do you find this assessment to be true? Discuss the possible reasons for this modern need for happy endings.

3. Radojčić includes characters from every religious and ethnic group (Muslims, Orthodox Christians, Catholics, and Jews) of the area in which *Homecoming* is set—and every one of them commits some sort of evil act, even if only a small one. Are moral crises inevitable in circumstances of war? Is it possible to preserve normal values under abnormal circumstances?

4. When Halid first sees Mira, his first and only love, he is touched and jealous over her tenderness toward her child. Is there any love left between them? What happens to romantic attachments in an environment in which basic human survival is threatened?

5. At the beginning of the book, when Halid steps off the bus, the bus driver yells, "Good luck to you, hero!" Discuss Halid as a heroic figure. He fought for the winning side and was wounded. Since his people were attacked he could be seen as a hero. What qualities does he possess that could define him as one? What makes a soldier a hero? Could Halid also be described as an antihero? Does Radojčić cast judgment on him one way or the other?

6. Halid shot Aida by accident. He had shot many people before and has seen many people die around him, and yet when he thinks of Aida's death he feels like a murderer. Why is Aida's death different?

7. Radojčić often uses nature and animals as metaphors for Halid's emotional life. Discuss your reaction to the hunt scene where a burrowing owl was killed. Why does Radojčić call it "an ignominy"? Is there an honorable way to kill animals? What about the horse tied to a stake, earlier in the novel? How do these animals foreshadow Halid's fate? The last part of the novel, after Halid loses all his money, occurs in the dark. Why do you think Radojčić sets it that way? How would it be different in daylight?

8. Halid's mother's touch "burns as bad as the bullet did." Why does his mother's affection hurt? How can affection from those who love us become unbearable? What could Halid have done in order to learn to accept care from others again?

9. Even after it is clear that his old friends have decided to kill him, Halid stays. Why doesn't he leave? Why doesn't he fight harder?

10. In the last few days of Halid's life, there seems to be no order. Things go from bad to worse. Were you surprised by the ending, or did you see it coming? Was Halid's path toward self-destruction a steady one?

11. One reviewer compared *Homecoming* to Gabriel García Márquez's *Chronicle of a Death Foretold*, a novel that logs, step by step, a man's murder. Santiago Nasar is stabbed by his friends: the entire town witnesses it. How do these novels compare? Do you think Radojčić wrote *Homecoming* with a similar purpose?

12. Radojčić is also a screenwriter. Is her experience as a writer of screenplays evident in the language of the novel? How would you envision this novel on the screen?